Men are for Christmas, not for life

Dedicated to my Mum, the best Mum in the world and the best friend I ever had and to my Dad, who was simply a legend.

Chapter 1 – We met

Chapter 2 – He married Helen, I married Andy, he divorced Helen

Chapter 3 – I divorced Andy, he met Dawn

Chapter 4 – Mindy moved in with us, I married Lenny

Chapter 5 – We lost touch, I divorced Lenny

Chapter 6 – We had a moment, I met Gavin and his friends

Chapter 7 – I travelled with Gavin, I split up with Gavin

Chapter 8 – I travelled alone, I met Brian

Chapter 9 – I married Brian, I divorced Brian, I finally got with Nick

Chapter 10 – The future

Chapter 1 We met

So here I am, a barren, orphaned woman aged fifty-three and three-quarters, sitting in the departure lounge at Southend airport, alone, waiting to board a plane to Alicante in Spain. My guts are playing up something terrible due to my fear of flying and my heart is hurting; not because of a pending heart attack I hope, but because a few days ago I moved out of the home that I've been sharing with the love of my life, Nick. I need to get away to clear my head. I really thought I'd cracked it this time, with three divorces under my belt and a fair amount of shit in between. I had been in a loving relationship, for the past two years, with my perfect man who I'd first met back in the early 1980's when I was the tender age of seventeen. What a life changing night that turned out to be.

I had left home at sixteen to go and travel the world. I had started by going to the Isle of Wight, which my Mum and Dad said was almost like going abroad because you had to go on a ferry to get there; bless them. I had come back to my hometown, good old

Basildon in Essex, to visit family and friends for the weekend and was having a girl's night out with two of my old school mates, Helen and Sharon. We were in a local pub, The Flying Childers, which was 'the' place to go at the time; all under-age, drinking Pink Lady, Lambrusco, Black Tower or some other exotic 1980's alcoholic beverage. The girls were wearing the latest fashionable clobber, ra-ra skirts, stilettos and caked in brightly coloured cheap make-up that had probably been nicked from the local Woolworths down the town and me, in my usual jeans, Indian cotton top purchased from Camden Market, my old faithful Hush Puppies and duffle coat and not a drop of make-up in sight. I had gone through a punk phase a year or so before and used to love going to a club, in nearby Rayleigh, called Crocs; named so, due to the large tacky plastic crocodile that was suspended from the ceiling. I was fascinated by the weird people that used to go there, not only punks but men in drag and all other sorts of crazy outfits. There were no doors on the cubicles in the toilets and they were, as we would say today, gender neutral which was unheard of then. The floor was always dirty and sticky, but nobody cared because it was packed with wonderful characters and the atmosphere was great. The bestselling drink was called a Rodney; nobody knew what was in it but after a couple of pints, that was you pissed for the next two days. Although the punk music was okay to dance and jump around to, get spat at to and headbutted to, I would get home and listen to a bit of Donny Osmond (my favourite to this very day) Dean Martin, Elvis, Al Green or Otis Redding. I hated wearing all that make-up, so I'd packed my ripped jeans and giant safety pins away and went back to being a hippy chick.

When Nick walked into the Flying Childers that night, he was with his mate Del. I instantly looked away from Del because he was a little bloke and obviously suffered from LBS (little bloke syndrome) and one of my rules is to never sleep with a man if you can see the top of his head when you dance with him. My Dad had the most severe case of LBS that I have ever known and, as much as I loved him, I could never have a relationship with an LBS victim. They annoy the fuck out of me; the way they walk with big strides and as though they've got a rolled-up carpet under each arm, their overconfidence and loudness, their love of flash cars and don't even get me started on how they eat peanuts! They put loads of nuts in the palm of their little hands, cup them, do the wanker sign and start chucking them, individually, into their big mouths with a quick flick and a speedy backwards jerk of their cocky little heads. Watching them makes my bum go funny and that isn't a good thing. On the dance floor they all tend to dance like Bruce Springsteen, and I can't stand him, all jerky movements and that, it's horrible. The thing that does me the most though, is the fact that they do love doing a bit of air guitar; that's seriously not nice to witness. British men should be tall and, by Christ, don't short men know it! They do everything in their power to look bigger, but they are not fooling me that's for sure. 'You are short, the Gods have been cruel, just accept it because you know it could have been far worse, so stop being so

5

bloody annoying and get over yourselves!'. Oops sorry, rant over.

I will be eternally grateful, however, for Del's shortness because my eyes went to Nick. He was tall, blonde, obviously visited the gym quite regularly but he seemed a bit shy and nervous which I found very appealing; I thought he was gorgeous. Unfortunately, so did Helen and it was soon apparent that I didn't stand a chance. He couldn't take his eyes off her and she was flirting with him like there was no tomorrow. I have since asked Nick why he went for her and not me, expecting him to say it was because I was a ginger haired fatty and a 'Plain Jane' dressed in old-fashioned clothes and she was a tiny, beautiful, trendy sex-goddess with gorgeous long dark hair. But no, he said that it was simply because she had bigger tits than me; he was nineteen years old and a tit-man, fair play. We had a brilliant time in the pub, despite the fact that not only did Helen and Nick get together, but Sharon and Del did too; I then became 'Jackie no-mates'. There was a band playing that night called 'Hedgehog'. Their music was a bit heavy for my liking, but they were so good

6

at getting everyone up dancing, which helped to make the night a proper award winner. That band are still playing the local pub circuit to this very day. They are the 'Rolling Stones' of Essex, good on them; they may be wrinkly now, but they've still got it.What really blew me away the most that night was Nick's pride and joy, his old Morris Minor that was parked outside. It was grey with a red interior; it was obviously well-loved and looked after and in great condition. My old Grandad had one when I was a kid, it was almost identical, and I had such fond memories of him letting me sit in the front; it made me feel all grown-up. I must have only been about eight years old at the time, but I remember loving the sound that the engine would make. Nick gave us all a lift home, but I lived the nearest so got dropped off first, thus, the Helen and Nick romance officially began. It's a good job it did really because they ended up getting married and had five kids in five years. Just think, if my tits had been bigger those five wonderful human beings may never have been born!

The day after I first met Nick, I returned to my waitressing job on the Isle of Wight. I thought about him every day and used to have untold scenario fantasies regarding the two of us; I was well and truly hooked. I had started working at the holiday camp in the April but it had to close for a few months at the end of the season, which was in October. I did not relish the thought of going back to Basildon and having to endure watching Helen and Nick's relationship flourish, so I rented a bedsit a few miles from the holiday camp, in Ryde. What a great little place that was; fully equipped, modern and it had a sea-view, perfect. I was supposed to live there until the following April when the camp was due to re-open, but I started to get bored and, for the first time in my life, a bit lonely. Most of the other holiday camp workers had gone back to their hometowns and the ones that were locals all lived on the other side of the island. None of us drove and public transport had almost come to a standstill, because it was winter, so I had nobody to play with. Just before Christmas two friends of mine, Charlie and Roger, travelled from Essex to the Isle of

Wight to stay with me for a few days. They had a car so the three of us went out exploring every day; it was nice to have a chauffeur and I was more than happy to be their tour guide. I showed them all the amazing places on the island; they had never been before and thankfully, they ended up sharing my views on what a wonderful place it was. As much as I enjoyed spending time with my friends, it made me realise how much I was missing my family and other friends, so I gave my flat up and travelled back to Basildon with them at the end of their stay and moved back home with my parents. I spent a lot of time with Charlie when I returned home, and he is still a good friend of mine today. This is amazing really because he proper broke my heart when I was only fifteen, which is one of the reasons why I had left home in the first place.

At the age of fourteen I joined the Basildon Youth Theatre. I have always been a bit of a drama queen and was the star pupil in my drama class at school, so it was a no-brainer that I should do drama as a hobby too. None of the boys ever fancied me at school, which is no surprise when I look back at the photos of me then; I was as rough as arseholes! All the boys just wanted to be my best mate because I was a tomboy and seen as just one of the lads. When I joined the youth theatre my confidence levels soared and for the first time ever, I felt as though I was socialising with people that could see just how excellent I actually was! It also helped that one of the most popular youth theatre members, Eddie, seemed to fancy me, how bizarre. He was dark haired, handsome, slim, trendy, slightly neurotic and extremely loud and camp, but he started flirting with me; he was acting like I was all sexy and that and I loved it. There was only one thing to do about this strange turn of events and that was to let him give me one of course. What an absolute disaster that was. Neither of us knew what to do and I was certainly not physically ready for a bunk-up. It's really not a good idea to lose your virginity before puberty has kicked in; I learned that the hard way. I must also mention that when I saw Eddie, many years later, he told me that after sleeping with me he'd realised that he was in fact gay. No hang on, it gets worse; after I packed Eddie in, I started going out with someone else from the youth theatre, Charlie, as in Charlie and Roger. The sex was a little bit better with Charlie because, a couple of years before, he'd had a girlfriend who he had impregnated just after they had left school. At least he'd had a bit of practice and there was, of course, absolutely no chance of me getting up the duff. Charlie and his ex-girlfriend had decided on a termination which was so sad because Charlie would have been a great dad; that turned out to be his one and only chance at it. He was three years older than me, had a car, a bright yellow Ford Escort, very Essex, had a job, money and I must say, or he'll never forgive me, was also very handsome and in a much more manly type of way than Eddie. We'd been seeing each other for a while but I was still only fifteen when Charlie asked me to have a weekend away with him. I knew that my Mum and Dad would not allow this, so I thought of a plan. I told my parents that Charlie would never be my boyfriend, just a close friend, because he was gay. Charlie was a little bit camp, so they fell for it and off we went for my first ever dirty weekend.

We went to a cheap bed and breakfast place in Walton-on-the-Naze, very classy and romantic don't you know! Looking back now I should have known something wasn't quite right when I popped out to get a newspaper, on our first morning there, and returned to find Charlie wearing my skirt and blouse. I just laughed it off, even though he looked better in the outfit than I did and didn't give it another thought. Charlie's best friend was a hairdresser called 'gay Tom', another clue. He was so nice but an over the top, flamboyant character who had a different shade of mad coloured hair every time that I saw him, and his outrageous clothes were always way too small to fit his large frame. Most weekends the three of us would go into London to various gay clubs. Most of these I liked because the music was always lively, very camp and great to dance to, handbag music it was called then; popular 1970's dance tunes mainly, the atmosphere was always good and I enjoyed it even more if there was a drag queen on. I still love the cutting, quick, bitchy humour of a good drag artist. We did a wrong-un one night though; we went to a club called 'Heaven' in the heart of London. The bouncers should never have let me in really because no fifteen-year-old girl needs to see men openly having sex in the, not so dark, corners of a club. I have always been very open-minded, but that was a step too far, even for me. One night, Charlie, Tom and I got on the train at Basildon for one of our London adventures and Tom went into the toilet. He was in there for the entire forty-five-minute journey to Fenchurch Street station. He then bursts out of the loo, in an over the top dramatic fashion, dressed in full drag. We all just laughed, not giving it a thought that if we'd come across the wrong crowd, we would have all had the shit kicked out of us. Behaviour like that was frowned upon by most people back then; it's so very different today, thankfully.

One evening Charlie introduced me to his new friend 'gay Roger' who he had met at work; no, I still didn't cotton-on. There's naive and there's as thick as pig shit and I know which category I'd put myself into, that's for sure. They had met a few months before and had already had a couple of weekends away together on, what he had told me, were business trips. I thought it was a bit odd going on work-related things at weekends but didn't analyse it too much. Roger was quite a bit older than us and a quiet and serious bloke, but I liked him. Although I really couldn't get my head around why we were socialising with someone so old; he was probably only about late twenties but that seemed old to me then. We met up with Roger for the next few weekends and Charlie seemed to talk about him a lot in-between our get-togethers.

I was with Charlie at his parent's house one evening when he informed me that he was going to be moving in with Roger, in his flat in Southend, the following week. What a result, we'd be able to spend whole nights together in Roger's spare bedroom and I told Charlie that I was proper excited about his plan. He was beginning to look a bit agitated at this point and then carried on explaining that he would be sleeping in Roger's bed. Cha-ching, finally the penny dropped. I was so shocked, why I don't know. I ran out of his house and cried all the way home. I had to pull myself together before I got in because, don't forget I had already told my Mum and Dad that Charlie batted for the other side; that'll teach me for telling porkies! I cried myself to sleep and the next day decided that I wanted to kill him and then myself. A slight overreaction and a tad dramatic some may say but I wasn't even sixteen to be fair, almost sixteen stone but still only fifteen years of age.

I thought long and hard about how I would kill us both and finally thought of a great idea. I would use my Chopper bike. I knew what time he used to walk up the steep hill every night on the way home from work, so I would wait at the top of the hill until I spotted him, start peddling, full speed ahead and hit him with my Chopper; not realising that the irony of a gay man being killed by a 'Chopper' was priceless. I figured that because I was a fat girl, the full force of my bulk, even without the bike, at high speed should kill him. Once I had squashed him, I would get back onto my Chopper and ride in front of the nearest oncoming car. Great plan, what could possibly go wrong? He'd be dead, so wouldn't be able to get rogered by Roger, another great bit of irony, and I would also be dead so would stop crying. It could have worked, I swear, but Charlie was just too quick. He did the best startled face ever as I came bombing towards him and threw himself out of the way, whilst I panicked when I could see it'd all gone horribly wrong and ended up face down on the pavement with bleeding hands and knees. The maddest part was that Charlie was proper shook up and I ended up consoling him! Oh well, all was forgiven, and we laugh about it still.

I never had any regrets about coming back early from the Isle of Wight with Charlie and Roger because I got to see Nick. I'd got my head round the fact that he was with Helen now, but it was just good to spend time with him again. In many ways we are so very different, Nick and I, but we have always had the ability to make each other laugh and we did plenty of that on my return. Soon after coming home I had decided to move out of my parent's house. This wasn't because there were any problems living with them, it was just that I had gotten the taste of independence and wanted more of the same. I was very happy living with my Mum and Dad in fact because they were great to be around, proper characters and they spoilt me and my sister something rotten. When I was a kid, I seemed to manage to get almost everything I wanted. All I had to say was that all my mates had, for example, a colour TV and like magic, one would appear. We were actually the first family in the street to get a colour telly which soon became apparent when every evening several kids would knock at our door to ask if they could see it. I used to get my Mum doing all sorts for me too. When I was thirteen years old, I asked my Mum if she would go down the town to buy me a record that 'all my friends had'. It was called Jilted John by Jilted John, but I thought it was called 'Gordon is a Moron' because that was a lyric that was repeated during the song. Off she went to the town but when she got back, she had a face like thunder. She said that she was never going into that record shop again because she'd made a fool of herself. She'd got confused and had asked for 'Norman is a Mormon'. Apparently, the record shop staff couldn't contain their laughter and she'd stomped out all red-faced.

Although me and my sister were spoilt, we were both encouraged from an early age, to get out there and earn some money. I was eleven when I started my morning and evening paper rounds and only twelve when I started babysitting the two little girls who lived next door, Tessa and Carly. Their Mum and Dad ran a local pub and they often worked late, so I would stay the night with them too. They were great kids; Tessa was eight years old and a proper cheeky little thing who often had me in stitches with her quick wit and funny outlook on life and the five-year-old Carly was super-cute, but a quiet and serious kid. I loved spending time with them and used to wish they were my little sisters. One night we all went upstairs to clean our teeth and have a wash before going to bed. There were two flannels draped over the sink, so the girls used them, and I grabbed the one that was on the side of the bath. I rinsed mine under the tap and was just about to put it on my face when a look of total horror crossed Tessa's face and she frantically shouted, 'Don't use that one, it's the fanny flannel'. Nice!

I actually loved being back in Basildon with my Mum and Dad for those few weeks because it gave me the chance to tell them all about the adventures that I'd had on the Isle of Wight. What I didn't like, however, was sleeping in my old bedroom again. My Mum actually gave birth to me in that room and I'd lost my virginity in there fourteen years later, so I thought that the only other big thing left in my life was death. Every night I was frightened to go to sleep in case I never woke up again! I slept much better when I moved in with my friend Sharon, not the little bloke lover Sharon from the night out when I'd first met Nick, this was another one.

There seemed to be so many Sharon and Tracy's about in Essex then, hence the mocking of the names via the famous Essex girl jokes that came about in 1991 and in the classic TV show 'Birds of a Feather' of course, that used the names for two of their main characters. The Sun newspaper were responsible for those never-ending jokes because they printed an article with the headline 'There are no virgins in Essex'. They had come to that conclusion after employing several good-looking young men to visit all of the British counties and asked them in which area they considered the girls to be the easiest to get their leg over with. Essex apparently came out on top, or on the bottom depending on how you look at it. Most of us Essex folk found the jokes funny, with the mocking of our white stilettos and handbags, love of kebabs after a night out and our East End of London type accents, but we didn't laugh at how there was a dramatic increase of rapes on the Fenchurch Street to Essex train line, due to many a thick Sun reader that actually believed that there really weren't any virgins in Essex!

Sharon was living in her Dad's three bedroom flat while he was staying at his latest girlfriend's place. Her Dad's name was Stan; he was a short, stocky bloke from gypsy descent and was a proper character and a real Jack the Lad. He always wore chunky gold jewellery, was oozing with confidence and had a wicked dry sense of humour. He was brought up in a caravan but moved into a bungalow, with his parents and siblings, when he was a teenager. His old Mum was adamant that they should never leave the caravan life so, on the day of the move, they drugged her up to enable them to get her into her new home, that they knew she would love, which she did. Stan's Dad was a very successful businessman and had made enough money to buy a big plot of land to build the bungalow on and then he concreted the rest out and turned it into a lorry yard. He owned shitloads of lorries too and his sons would drive them for him. Stan loved the ladies but seemed to get fed up with them after a while and now, sadly, lives alone in his old age.

I moved into the box room of the flat, Sharon had the middle room and Bill, a sixty-nine-year-old blind man, was in the biggest room. Bill had worked for Stan's Dad for many years, right up until he got ill and lost his eyesight and the family were still taking care of him. What an odd combo of people we were, but it worked a treat and we all lived together in perfect harmony. Sharon did all the cooking, I was a terrible cook and Bill, in his defence, was blind, so would have found it a bit difficult. Sharon did all the housework because she said she liked doing it. Apparently, I wasn't all that at buying the shopping either, so that became her task too. Happy days. All I had to do was go to work, greet my friendly drug dealer at the door once a week, smoke cannabis, party a lot, sleep with whoever I liked, whenever I liked and wind Sharon up a few evenings a week by blasting out my music, which she hated, when she was trying to have a nice peaceful bath. What was her problem? Who doesn't just love listening to the 'Cabaret' album accompanied by an out of tune Basbird singing very loudly along with Liza Minnelli!

During that time Sharon and I went on holiday to Spain together. We had such a laugh that week and met shitloads of blokes; Sharon was a good girl, but I wasn't. We were sitting around the pool one day, with a group of London lads that we had met, when I suddenly got a terrible poo pain. I told everyone that I was just popping back to mine and Sharon's room for a minute. When I got there the whole world seemed to fall out of my arse. I must have been on that loo for ten minutes before I felt confident enough to get off. I tidied myself up and returned to the pool area.

When I got there, I bent over and started to rearrange the towel on my sunbed and realised that everyone had started laughing. I couldn't understand why; I hadn't heard anyone say anything funny. Sharon then said, 'I bet you feel better after that don't ya?'. I was mortified and thinking that the clean-up job hadn't been as successful as I'd thought. When I looked at my bikini covered bum, I saw that there was a mark, a beautiful big bright red oblong mark from the toilet seat, deeply embedded into my flesh. How embarrassing! I may just as well of come back with a sign on my chest saying, 'I've got bad guts'.

I have always suffered with my guts and feel strangely proud that I've managed to shit myself in seven different countries to date, excluding the two times I've done it in the UK. In fact, the UK incidents were probably the worst of all. The first time was after eating some dodgy salmon which made me, quite literally, explode twelve hours later, when I was tucked up in bed with one of my husbands and our dog. I got a horrendous pain and vomited, with great force, onto the dog who was sound asleep in my arms, but the husband was snuggled in behind me so trust me, he got the worst of it. The other time was outside the council offices in a very busy Basildon town centre on a Saturday afternoon. I was with my Mum and youngest niece, then about ten, and without warning it just happened and it was bad; no idea what I'd eaten but it had gone through me like a fucking train. Even when I'm going through a slim phase, I am still a fat bird trapped inside a skinny bird's body, so I never wear clothes that show my bum off. For some unknown reason, on that fateful day, I had put on a pair of light green short trousers and a short vest top. My Mum looked at me as though I'd gone mad when I suddenly leant up against the wall outside as though I had a firing squad in front of me. When I told her what had happened, she said, 'Why have you done that'? I wanted to say, 'Oh, I'm sorry, I don't know Mum, for attention perhaps?!!!', but I thought better of it, I didn't want a clip round the earhole to add to the horror of the situation. It was terrible, none of us had a cardigan to hide my shame so I had to walk into the council and beg the reception staff to use their toilet and then stand in there, naked from the waist down, while I washed myself and my trousers in the sink. What a fucking nightmare that one was!

Sharon had a younger brother, Grant, who'd had a pretty bad cringey moment just the week before we had gone on our holiday. We were all at a party and Grant thought that it would be funny to light one of his farts; what the fuck made him think that would be a good idea, I will never know. He soon regretted it though because it went horribly wrong. He dropped his trousers, put a lighter near his bum and as he let one go, a five feet long blue flame shot out across the room! He burst out laughing, but then as quick as the flame had shot out, it shot back in again and disappeared right into his bum-hole; he stopped laughing then! It actually burnt his insides and he had to go to the hospital, silly sod; he never did that party-piece again.

Sharon and I have been the best of friends since senior school. She's a special, unique, larger than life character, so much fun to be around and has got a heart of gold. My Dad used to call her his 'rough diamond.' If she likes you, she'll do anything for you, day or night, but if she doesn't like you, well, good luck with that one! We met in odd circumstances when we were both twelve years old. One of the school bullies had managed to lift me up and place the hood of my sweatshirt onto a coat hook in the changing rooms of the school gym. I was just hanging there with my feet dangling off the ground, the collar of my top cutting into my chin(s) which was almost strangling me. She was just about to start giving me a dig when in walked my Sharon, soon to be my good friend and hero. I'd obviously seen the famous Sharon around school, she was in a couple of my classes, but I'd never dared talk to her. She was one of the popular girls and a proper hard nut, but never a bully; in fact, she hated the bullies which soon became apparent. She was so cool, she walked over to me, lifted me off the hook and then gave the bully a gob full of abuse

27

and warned her that if she ever touched me again, she'd kill her. Thanks to Sharon I never got any stick at school ever again. She was like my bouncer and a very entertaining one at that.

I could have done with befriending Sharon when I had first started school really because I had to endure my fair share of bullying in the infants and juniors too. Looking back, I was a poor little cow really. I was always so fat and ill and trust me, my speech impediment didn't help one bit either. My leg was in plaster for months after the hospital had broken my knee bone to test the marrow for cancer. They hadn't given me a wheelchair because my Mum said I'd be more comfortable in my old pushchair. She'd wheel me to school in it, which used to make me so embarrassed at six years old but even worse, my classmates would have a field day pushing me around the playground at full speed during breaktime. There was a free-standing brick wall outside, that was used as a goal for when the fit kids played football but it was also often used to entertain the masses by pushing me into it and pissing themselves laughing as my plastered leg hit it. This would make my whole body leave the pushchair, I'd then faceplant the bricks and land sideways onto the ground. Nice one!

After becoming Sharon's friend, we used to walk part of the way home from school together and she always wanted to come back to my house for a while, but I used to like going to hers; she often got her own way and came to mine a lot. We had very different homes. Mine was quiet and chilled because my Dad was often working abroad, my sister worked long hours in London and my Mum worked at home on her beloved Singer sewing machine, making clothes for various companies, which she enjoyed but she must have been a bit lonely so she loved it when I brought friends home. My Dad was away for months at a time, she never drove, she had no real friends to speak of and her family, who were her world, all lived miles away, so she rarely got to see them. Poor Mum. When I look back it breaks my heart;

she had such a sad life when my sister and I were young. If only she had passed her driving test, then her life would have been so different; she could have got out and about so much more. My Dad always had a car, but when he was away it used to be parked at the front of our house, with a cover over it, just sitting there doing nothing; what a terrible waste. Even when my Dad was at home it must have been hard for her because they liked doing such different things. He loved listening to his rock and roll music, going to pubs and clubs, getting pissed and jiving. He was an absolutely brilliant dancer and over the course of many years, managed to teach all of his sisters, his daughters and even his two eldest granddaughters how to jive. He used to be able to jive with two women at the same time, one hand each, very impressive and great to watch. My Mum, however, liked her opera, especially her beloved Mario Lanza, going to the theatre and simply visiting her loved ones. She adored Sharon's visits and thought she was such a caring, funny girl and always made a fuss of her, but she didn't approve of Sharon's family however, but I thought they were the bollocks.

Sharon's Mum was one of a kind, my Sue. I feel so sad thinking about her because she died way too young and it was a huge loss to everyone that knew her when she passed away, or 'went home' as she used to say people had done when they'd died. Sue always looked great; she was tall and slim, used to bleach her hair and wear tarty clothes but they looked lovely on her. She wore a fair bit of make-up and put it on well, bright red lips and matching long nails, she had tats at a time when women just didn't have tattoos, she was always dripping in gold and didn't take any shit from men, women or children.

Sharon's parents had separated a couple of years before, leaving just her, Grant and Sue living in the family home. The divorce settlement stated that Sue was to keep all of the furniture in the home, so her Dad turned up with a chain-saw and cut everything into two, including the television and sofa, but excluding the kids' stuff, because he believed that he should of got half of it. Terrible thing to happen, but they never seemed to be phased by it, they just got new stuff and carried on with life. Sue's house was beautiful. It was always spotlessly clean, full of quirky ornaments and quite often, quirky people too. Sometimes when Sharon and I arrived at Sue's after school, she'd be sat in her lounge with a few of her male black friends and they'd all be smoking odd smelling fags and laughing a lot!

Sue was also a very spiritual woman and used to randomly say things to me that there was no way on Earth she could possibly have known about and then advise me on what to do. Once she advised me to put surgical spirit on my face to get rid of my teenage spots. Unfortunately, I misheard and used white spirit instead which proper burnt my face! She had an Ann Summers party when they first came about, so thanks to Sue, before I'd even seen a willy, I thought that they were all gonna be massive and black! I witnessed Sharon and Sue have a full-blown fistfight once; after about two minutes of them punching and kicking the shit out of each other Sue seemed to be winning, so Sharon pulled a clever move by whipping the towel off her Mum, leaving her standing there naked. I was sitting on the sofa with Grant watching all of this happen right in front of me; he was laughing about it up until Sue was standing there starkers, he then got up and kicked Sharon so hard up the arse that she literally flew across the room. That was that, fight over. I was really shaken up because I'd never seen anything like it before, but they all made up really quickly so that helped me to pull myself together. They were a mad lot, but they fascinated and amused me, and I was touched by the way they took me into their hearts.

Talking of willies, the first real one that I ever saw, would you believe, was at a school for special needs children when I was just thirteen years old. Helen, who later married Nick, and I were also very good friends whilst at school. My Mum thought the world of Helen, but she said that she used to worry when I knocked about with her because we always seemed to get into some sort of trouble. Nine times out of ten this was my fault, but Helen always got the blame because she was a popular girl and looked a bit tarty and I was an ill geek; proof that appearances can be deceptive. We were at school one morning when I talked Helen into bunking off with me. We snuck out of the school gates and were wandering around aimlessly, when we found ourselves outside the local bingo hall, so I made her go in with me. I was a spoilt little cow and always had money on me because my parents used to let me keep the family allowance money that the government kindly gave us on a weekly basis. I had always wanted to go to bingo because my Dad used to say how good it was. He was working in Saudi Arabia for months at a time back then and he told us how he used to organise bingo nights for his work mates for a bit of entertainment. They were all totally fucked off and bored working away from home, because there was no alcohol or women to make them happy. My

34

Dad was always the bingo caller, but he used to wind them all up by saying things like 'Two fat ladies, number 27' or 'Kelly's Eye, number 14'. That was his LBS coming out for sure!

Unfortunately, the staff at the bingo hall took my money and let me and Helen in, but then they phoned the school and grassed us up. We were both sent to see the Head of Year teacher and poor Helen, who I had led astray, got a proper big telling off and a few detentions, but I just got a gentle talking to. The teacher told me that he thought it would be for the best if I stopped being friends with Helen because she was a troublemaker and suggested that I did some voluntary work at the special needs school, during the lessons that I didn't really need to attend. I was always poorly with my asthma and arthritis, so I used to just sit doing nothing during lessons like Physical Education and Wood and Metal work. From that day on I would walk to the other school and help them out. My main duties were in the classroom that was for the severely disabled children; most of whom were doubly incontinent. At just thirteen years of age, I was changing nappies of kids that were, mostly, older than I was! So, the first time I saw a willy it was covered in poo, no lie, how bad is that? Sending a kid to tidy other kids up! However, I must point out that I loved my time working in that school; I enjoyed every aspect of the work and found it very rewarding. The teachers said that I was very good at it and I considered taking it up as a career, but my need to travel put an end to that idea.

When I was working at the school, I was given an envelope which I was told to give to my parents. It contained sheets of stamps; not postage stamps but they were that size. The idea was to stick one of the stamps next to the postage stamp when posting something. It was to promote a message from the school, like a free way of advertising I assume. My Mum was a bit of a hoarder and kept the stamps, in the 'messy drawer', for many years. She came across them in December 2011 and thought it would be a great idea to stick them on her Christmas cards because they looked pretty. Unfortunately, the message on the stamps was no longer appropriate because it stated 'Help Spastics'. Several family members phoned me to ask if my Mum had lost the plot. Fuck knows what the postmen thought. Oopsy Daisy!

Helen and Nick used to come to all of mine and Sharon's mad parties at our flat and they'd regularly attend the legendary card and board game nights at my Mum and Dad's too; I would even the numbers up by bringing along whatever bloke I was seeing at the time. We all used to have such a laugh together and Helen and Nick really were like part of our family, we all loved them both lots. One night, at my Mum and Dad's, they announced their engagement and informed us that the wedding was booked for that September. I was so happy for them, but the news did hurt my heart; I didn't show it though, forever the actress. Why I was upset is beyond me because my life was great. I was full of confidence and fun, loved living with my Sharon, I had passed my driving test, had a car, a job in a local café that I enjoyed, no money worries and I always had a bloke on the go. However, I continued to compare all my boyfriends to Nick; he was the only one that I'd ever really wanted, sad but true. After hearing about the engagement, I had to get away, just like I am doing now thirty-five years later, to try to get him out of my head, so I headed back to the Isle of Wight. I hate to admit it, but it didn't work all those years ago and it probably won't work this time either!

Chapter 2 He married Helen, I married Andy, he divorced Helen

Nick, like me but two years earlier, was born and brought up in Basildon; it was then a new town, in Essex. It was built in the 1950's by the council, to accommodate the overspill of the very overcrowded Dagenham area. Nick's parents, like mine, moved into their brand-new council house which they were offered simply because one of them worked in the Basildon area. How times have changed eh? It's not so easy to get a council place now; they're like gold-dust! My parents were newlyweds in 1954 and renting a room in a house owned by, what turned out to be lifelong friends, a wonderful Indian family in Battersea, London. They loved living there but needed their own place really, so my Mum left her dressmaking job in London and got a new one in Basildon. Within a matter of weeks, they were asked which type of accommodation they would like in Basildon. They could have had a flat, bungalow or a house that was detached, semidetached, mid or end-terraced and they were allowed to say how many bedrooms they wanted, from one to four! They went for a mid-terrace place, with three bedrooms. They didn't even have any kids and got a brand-new, three bedroom home just like that; mad innit! Good on them and the hundreds of other young couples that took advantage of that fantastic offer, but when you compare those days to now, it is a bit depressing. Our housing situation has gone proper downhill mainly because, years later, we were told that we could buy our council properties and were strongly encouraged to do so in fact, which so many people did of course.

My parents were absolutely thrilled with their new home and were overwhelmed by how much living space they had, for the first time ever. They had both lived their whole lives in crowded homes and, apart from their short time in Battersea, neither of them had ever even had a bedroom! My Dad was the only boy, he had seven sisters and my Mum was the only girl, with five brothers. Their parents had to have their own room of course and their siblings were all crammed into the remaining bedrooms, top-to-tail, so they had always had to sleep on the sofa in the lounge. My Mum used to say that it really didn't bother her but, as her brothers got older, it sure as hell bothered them. If they had been out with the lads and had managed to pull a bird, as they used to say back in the day, they would obviously want to get them back home for a snog on the sofa, but my Mum was always on there, with a smug look on her face apparently, according to my uncles. She said that contraception was not as accessible then, so it was thanks to her that there was never an unwanted pregnancy in the family. My Dad's situation, however, worked in his favour. When his parents and sisters were all tucked up in bed, he had the whole of the downstairs to himself so, for him, it was like having his own bachelor pad. My Dad, being the little bugger that he was, took full advantage of that, I should imagine. It's so funny how things change so much from generation to generation because we think we are proper hard done by now if the children haven't got a bedroom each.

Nick was the youngest of five children, he had two brothers and two sisters. They were a happy and loving family, his Dad worked at the Fords in Dagenham most of his working life and his Mum had various jobs including being a store detective in the local Woolworths, which she did for many years. They later purchased and ran a successful convenience store, come off licence in Benfleet, a couple of miles outside of Basildon. His Dad died quite young, but his Mum is still going strong to this very day. Nick's parents were totally devoted to each other, so it was very hard for his Mum when his Dad passed away. She is a lovely lady and I always manage to get her to reminisce when I visit; she loves talking about her past and I love hearing about it. Nick also enjoys listening to his Mum's stories and has said that he finds out new information about her whenever the three of us manage to get together. I think that it is very important to 'interview' our elderly loved ones to try to get as much information out of them while they are still with us; let's face it, when they die, they take their untold stories with them. My parents loved nothing more than getting their old photo albums out, which my Mum kept in very organised albums in date order and everything, dating back to 1892. She would enjoy telling us about the people in the photographs and the full circumstances in which they had been taken; one single picture could start off a ten-minute story, it was great. When their grandchildren came along, they were in their element because they had another generation to tell their wonderful stories to.

Nick and I went to the same infants, junior and senior schools because our two families lived in the same catchment area. I have no memory of ever seeing or talking to Nick, nor him me, but I suppose as kids our two-year age gap made us worlds apart then. In Nick's words he was 'a right little sod' and was always up to mischief and forever being told off at home and at school. He and his best mate, little Del, used to enjoy their fishing, newting, dressing up in their donkey jackets, tricky kipper hats and Doc Martins and riding around the town on their bikes seeing what naughty things they could get up to next; a favourite being trying to pinch fags out of the local off licence. Little buggers!

Another favourite place of Nick and Del's, and mine by the way, was a nearby large field that was next to our junior school. It was basically a dumping ground for local builders who used to go there daily to chuck all their old shit in the field. Old broken pallets mainly, but also knackered planks of wood with rusty old nails sticking out of them, scaffold poles and any old tools they no longer wanted like hammers with half a handle, blunt saws, wobbly pliers and the like. Dozens of kids used to go to this death-trap after school and at weekends. We used to build little houses and often managed to get the structures up to three stories high, quite clever really. Often, you'd hear a blood curdling scream from someone that had trodden on a rusty nail or almost cut a finger off with a saw and there'd be several screams when the buildings would inevitably collapse, which would conclude with everybody falling from a great height. If all of that wasn't bad enough, if it got cold or dark, we'd start a fire that would always end up getting out of control. Nobody seemed to stress about this, even though there was no water about, we'd just extinguish the fast growing inferno by bashing it with one of the unpopular kids coats and if that didn't work, we'd all pile in and hit it with planks of wood until the flames disappeared, job done.

It was utter madness, but we used to have so much fun and as far as I know, nobody actually ever got killed there. When me and Nick recently reminisced about this place we were in fits of laughter and talked about how unbelievably different life is now due to the health and safety laws. I often crap on about how much I hate the way that kids of today spend all of their free time on electronic devices, but let's be honest, they are much safer doing that; no chance of them getting blood poisoning, falling to their deaths or getting burnt alive when they are on their iPads.

Nick has always admired the female form, he wasn't that keen on their company, but would put up with it if it meant him seeing them naked or better still, actually giving them one. He had trouble chatting up girls; he was extremely shy and not at all confident. He never would have had the courage to approach Helen, when they met, but he'd thought that she was her older sister, Tracy, who Nick had known from school. Nick discovered porn at a very early age, he loves it all; mags, videos and he strongly agrees with the theory that the internet was invented solely to watch pornography. He enjoys playing with his willy and has done so since the age of ten. One of the happiest moments of his life, was when he learned how to wank. He said that he's surprised that he ever left his bedroom again after that wonderfully life changing day. He swears blind that his willy got so big because he'd given it so much attention and exercise, almost every day of his life in fact. His love of sex was his main reason for wanting to get married. Helen and I were still very good friends, but I was also close enough to Nick to ask, after the announcement of their engagement, why he had proposed to Helen. He told me that he hadn't; Helen's sister Tracy and her partner Den had just got engaged and set a date, so Helen suggested they make it a double wedding. The sisters were happy because they had a Dad and a step-dad, so there would be no arguments when it came to who was going to give them away, they could do one each and Nick was happy because I quote 'I want to get married, so that I can have sex whenever I want it.'

What an excellent statement that was, a load of old shit and wishful thinking of course, but still a beauty. We all know that if you want sex whenever you want it, don't get married!

September came around way too quickly. I was still waitressing in the Isle of Wight and had no intention of going to Helen and Nick's wedding. I had even turned down her offer of being one of her bridesmaids. Not only would I have found it difficult, seeing them get married, but I really was having a great time and loving the holiday camp life this second time around. I did enjoy the first season that I had worked there but I was only sixteen then, which may have been a bit young to leave home really. I'd often get homesick and I didn't appreciate what a good laugh it could be then, nor did I embrace the freedom that I'd had. It was a regular holiday camp the first season, with families and couples mainly, but sometimes a group of lads would show up and us female workers made the most of that! There were never any groups of girls; I don't think it was the norm for girls to go away together then, much to the male workers disgust. The camp was situated on the Military Road that runs along the Isle of Wight's coastline; it's a beautiful part of the world. There was nowhere to go of an evening after work, except for the camp's clubhouse. There was a pub about a ten minute walk down the road, but it was always half empty and had very little atmosphere. It was always advisable to go and socialise with the campers anyway because if you got to know them, they tended to give you a bigger tip at the end of their holiday. The week of your birthday, you had to get up onto a chair in the dining room and all the staff and campers would sing to you. Although that may have been a bit embarrassing, your tips would always go up dramatically that week, so it was worth it. There were ten of us waitresses so we each had a birthday every ten weeks; naughty but clever and necessary because our wages were shit so we needed to boost them up somehow. We got free bed and board of course but our rooms were unbelievably small. Mine was only five-foot wide by eight-foot long and all it had in it was a single bed and a tiny sink in the corner. It was quite a walk from our tiny homes to get to the toilet and shower block and there were always big fuck-off spiders in the loos. I used to be petrified of them because I thought they might be poisonous. Well they could have been, I was 'sort of abroad' remember!

My phobia of spiders came from having witnessed someone get a nasty bite from one when I was on a school trip a couple of years before I'd left home. Apart from the horror of watching one of my friends almost die after she had been bitten, it was an amazing trip. I went away for three weeks on the SS Uganda. It was a cruise ship back then, in the late 1970's, but became a hospital ship a few years later and was used during the Falklands War. The trip started with a flight to Malta where we got onto the ship; after seeing some of the Maltese sights of course. When I said 'got onto' the ship, I actually meant 'dragged on' out of the small boat that had got us to the ship's side entrance, by several, possibly Asian, blokes that all had very angry faces. Their uniforms were filthy and they proper stunk of body odour. We were all frightened because they couldn't speak English and were screaming at us in their native tongues, whilst doing very dramatic hand signals. Apart from the scary staff, I loved that trip. I saw some spectacular parts of the world and vowed that I would see lots more of it one day, when I was old enough. We went to Italy, Greece, Israel and Egypt before flying back to the UK; what a wonderful experience, I was a lucky girl. I was fascinated by the ancient ruins in Italy and Greece, thought the pyramids had the wow factor but Israel was my absolute favourite place; perhaps it's that Jewish blood in me! When I was in Israel, that first time, it was still illegal for women to visit the 'Wailing Wall' but even seeing it from a distance fascinated me and I was overwhelmed by the 'Garden Tomb' and the 'Dome of the Rock'; Jerusalem is such an amazing place, it's one of my favourites.

I was always such an adventurous child, which my parents loved, because my sister wouldn't even go on day trips when she had been at school, she was a quiet, homely girl and a bit of a wuss. I had already been to Wales for a week with the school, a few months before the cruise, where I had done hiking, abseiling, horse riding and had crawled through pitch black caves. The school never seemed to worry about my ill health where trips were concerned, they happily took my parent's money and let me join in with everything; a bit naughty of them really but I had a great time and only ever got taken ill once while on one of my many trips. That was in Wales; I had a severe asthma attack because one of the teachers had driven me half a mile outside of the farm we were staying on, kicked me out of the car and told me that I had to walk back on my own. That would have been okay(ish) if it hadn't of been pitch black and freezing cold. There were no streetlights on the country road and the bastard hadn't even given me a bloody torch! I had been cheeky to him earlier that day, but he waited until it had got dark before dishing out my punishment. All I remember is feeling very cold and scared, as I watched the lights on his car disappear into the distance; then I panicked and couldn't breathe. I woke up in hospital but I'm not sure how I got there but they released me the next day and I happily cracked on with my trip. When I got home I told my Mum what had happened and all she said was 'I bet you regret being cheeky to the teacher now, don't you?' followed by 'I bet you won't do that again in a hurry, will you?'. She should have been a counsellor, my Mum!

She could be quite hard at times with me, my sister and my Dad. He was forever telling us how much he loved us, especially when he was pissed. We would always say it back, but my Mum never would. He'd often do his nut at her about it, but she'd always respond by saying 'I told you that I loved you in 1954 and I'm not one to repeat myself'. She never once told her daughters or granddaughters that she loved them, well not in English anyway, her excuse being that her generation felt uncomfortable being soppy and she felt no need to state the bleedin' obvious. We were her family, so we knew that she loved us, no need to keep on about it! When we were little, she used to send us up to bed and then come to tuck us in soon after. Occasionally, before she left the room, she'd turn the light off and quietly say 'Gute nacht, ich liebe dich' which is 'Good night, I love you' in German! She spoke a bit of German due to her several trips to Austria to visit her sister-in-law's family, so she must have felt somehow more comfortable saying it in a different language, strange innit?

I am forever saying 'regret is a wasted emotion' because it is. However, there is just one single thing that I do regret doing in my life, so far anyway. When I arrived at the holiday camp for the very first time, it was a Tuesday and all of us new season staff were sat around a large table in the dining room area. I think the idea was to start getting to know each other before the first holidaymakers were due to arrive, on the Saturday. We were all so young and, for most of us, it was our first job away from our loved ones. Most of the staff were from the north of England because, so they informed me, it was very difficult to find any work in their hometowns. They had been forced to come to the camp to be able to earn a living, very sad. I felt so sorry for them, my situation was much different. I was there just because I wanted to travel the world. In the south of England, at the time, you could literally walk out of one job and into another the next day, no problem. I knew this because I had done it myself a couple of times in the past few months, since I had left school.

Everyone seemed to be smoking except for me because I didn't like the smell of it. I had just spent the first sixteen years of my life living with parents who smoked a lot and I used to hate it. I remember as a kid, sitting in the back of my Dad's car with my sister, often on long journeys, begging my Mum to open the window because they were both puffing away on their cigarettes; the car was full of smoke and I couldn't breathe properly. Bear in mind that I was an asthmatic child, just to make it even worse. If my Mum ever gave in to my moaning about the lack of oxygen and opened a window, my Dad would say 'Turn it in Rose, shut that bloody window, you are letting all the heat out.' They would both then light-up again because they'd had a tiff and were stressed out, so I learnt that it was best to just suffer in silence.

When we look back on old cine films or videos, at every family get-together, almost every adult in the room would have a fag in their hand; even the ones holding newborn babies and you see the children running around with their hands above their heads, breaking through the thick clouds of smoke like it was their favourite game. Utter madness it seems now, but nobody gave it a second thought years ago. Despite saying all that, when one of my new holiday camp colleagues said to me 'Don't you smoke?', like I was some sort of freak, I said a really stupid thing. So, here it comes, the line that I have regretted saying from that day onwards, I said 'Yes, of course I do but I have run out of fags,' she replied 'Oh you should of said silly, you can have one of mine'. It was a menthol cigarette and it tasted absolutely disgusting but I smoked it anyway, just to be like the rest of my new friends. I have gone through my entire life without being controlled by man, woman or child, but my smoking addiction has controlled me every day since the first time I put that first horrible fag into my mouth.

I have used every 'stop smoking' product known to mankind, patches, nicotine gum, sweets and sucky things. I have been hypnotised and tried acupuncture, but still I continue to be a dirty smoker. Apart from that nasty life changing moment, I have very fond memories of that holiday camp.

The second season there was so much better, even though it had been turned into a SAGA holiday camp for the over 55's, so sleeping with the campers was no longer an appealing option. However, the old pub down the road had been turned into a club (no hang on, a 'disco' I should say) during the past year so that livened up the evenings somewhat. I still used to visit my campers in the clubhouse but now only during the weeknights because, obviously, I enjoyed the weekend disco a lot more. I had to learn how to do ballroom dancing that year, again, to maximise my tips. The original band, who were great and used to play all modern stuff, had been replaced by three old geezers called the 'Reg Hoskins Trio'. There was a singer, a guitarist and a drummer that used to love using that brush thing to slide across the drums, rather than actually banging them with a stick; he used to proper annoy me, I don't know why, it was a teenage thing perhaps. I could do all the dances me; the quickstep, waltz, foxtrot but my favourite was the tango because it was so dramatic. I really enjoyed it, all us young workers did, but we never spoke about our new dance moves when we went to the disco and bopped around to the latest 'Frankie Goes to Hollywood' or 'Pet Shop Boys' hits. Ballroom dancing has become more fashionable now, thanks to 'Strictly Come Dancing' being on the telly, but it was a very uncool pastime when I was a teenager.

A birthday card from Helen was delivered to the camp for me in the August because it really was, genuinely, my birthday this time! She had put a letter inside, begging me to attend their wedding and said she would be choked if I wasn't there. My parents, sister and brother-in-law were all going to the whole day of the wedding and I was well overdue a visit home, so I decided to go. It was a beautiful wedding and was held in the only local church that had an aisle wide enough for four people to walk down, side by side. The reception was a good laugh too. I was so glad that I went, and I knew, from that day on, I had to get a fucking grip of myself and stop thinking about Nick in that way. On the strength of that, soon after, I decided to move back home and in with my parents again. A lot of my friends had also got married and Helen was now pregnant, so I thought I'd better also go down that same route. I often say, 'You can't be happy all your life, you have got to get married at some point!'. Sadly, Helen had a miscarriage three months after their wedding and had to stay in hospital for a couple of days. It was early

December, so Nick and I decided to go and get a nice tree and some decorations, to make their new flat look all Christmassy for when she was discharged. Our efforts were not in vain because she was delighted when she got back and it lifted her spirits after the terrible ordeal of losing, what would have been, their first child.

At that time Nick worked for a television hire company as a delivery and repair man. He'd managed to get a good deal on renting a flat above one of the company shops, which was a right result. It was a big old place and I had helped them get it done up because it had been in a right state when they first got it but looked nice after a bit of elbow grease and cheap wallpaper and paint. I spent a lot of time with my newly married friends and as much as I enjoyed their company, at times I felt like a bit of a spare-part and knew I needed to get myself a husband to create a happy four.

In the new year, whilst on a girlie night out with Helen, I met Andy, thought that he would do nicely, thank you very much, and married him the following year. He was a good-looking man, tall, looked a sporty type even though he so wasn't, and he had a magnificent mass of thick, curly fair hair. Andy and I soon became Helen and Nick's best friends and occasional babysitters of their first born, Nick junior, who was the spitting image of his handsome dad. A year later, they were blessed with a beautiful daughter, Chloe.

Andy and I had decided to wait a few years before having kids because we were buying our house and wanted to get it all done up first. It was handy because Andy was a qualified painter and decorator and great at DIY, so we only ever had to find the money for materials. He was so talented but never continued with his career as a decorator with the council because he said they used to make him work at speed and he was a perfectionist, so hated not doing the job to the best of his ability. He ended up working in a timber yard as a general dogsbody, what a waste, but he seemed happy enough with his job so that was one of the few things that I didn't nag him about. He really never brought out the best in me. I used to moan and nag him almost constantly, most of the time for no reason at all, and was forever slagging his parents off, I am ashamed to say. I had just got my first job in retail and was always much happier at work than I was at home. I was forever doing unpaid overtime, just so I didn't have to go home, which is probably why I got promoted to deputy manager within the first year of employment. We only ever seemed to laugh when we were with Helen and Nick. We spent so much time with them, and I think we were both quite jealous of their relationship and how happy they seemed to be. They had managed to get a three-bedroom council house, not in the nicest part of Basildon but they seemed so content with what they had and with their ever-growing family.

Sophia arrived next, Helen and Nick's third child, and she was just as gorgeous as her older two siblings. She was a chubby, happy, healthy and very contented baby but when she was just five months old, the worst thing imaginable happened. It was the early hours of the morning and our phone rang. There were no mobile phones back then, only landlines, so Andy had to run down the stairs to answer it. He sounded upset; it was Helen on the phone, she was informing him that Sophia had slept past her usual bottle time and when they went to check on her it was immediately apparent that she had died. Nick tried desperately to resuscitate her until the ambulance arrived, but she had gone. When we arrived at their house, they had just taken Sophia away and I believe, a big part of Helen and Nick's hearts with her. It is still, to this very day, the saddest thing that I have ever been a part of. There was a grave opposite where Sophia was laid to rest, which stated on the headstone: the baby's name, died at one week old and the word 'WHY'. The church made them remove that headstone because it was, apparently, too upsetting for people to see. How bad is that of the church, not respecting what that baby's loved ones wanted on his headstone? There were no human rights then, more's the pity. Yes, of course it was upsetting to look at, but I personally thought that the word 'WHY' pretty much sums up how we all feel about a baby's death.

Sophia's death changed so many people's lives in lots of ways, Helen and Nick's mainly of course. Neither of them were ever the same again and their relationship certainly wasn't. Unfortunately, they didn't manage to grieve together and started to lead almost separate lives. Helen became a smoker at the age of twenty-four, way too old to start that habit, and seemed to only be happy when she was out with her mates, partying and drinking lots, leaving Nick at home with the kids, battling with his grief, alone. Nick became a very serious bloke and started working more. He was pretty nonstop before Sophia died but he was now doing even longer hours. They decided not to have any more children but when they went to the doctors to enquire about sterilisation, Helen was already pregnant. Baby Emma came along a few months later, followed by Brandon sixteen months after that. When Brandon was a few months old, I returned home from work one evening to be informed by Andy that Nick would be moving in with us that night. We had two spare bedrooms, so no problem accommodating him, but I said, 'What the hell, he's got a wife and four kids at home!'. Andy went on to explain that Nick had found out that Helen had been having an affair and that it wasn't the first one that she'd had either; so sad. With her regular girlie nights out I wasn't too shocked, but it did amaze me how she found the energy to have lovers, being a mum to so many kids. So, Nick become our lodger. It wasn't an ideal situation because I was in love with him, but I was married. Nick was heartbroken, so to become his best friend ever was my aim and I succeeded. Nick divorced Helen.

Chapter 3 I divorced Andy, he met Dawn

Nick settled in with me and Andy okay; we hardly used to see him really because we were all out at work all day during the week and he often went out after work to visit other friends and his family. Most weekends Nick stayed at Helen's with the kids while she went out on the lash. He was sort of like a babysitter in a way, but he didn't mind, he just loved spending time with his kids. Occasionally, he brought the kids to stay with us. It was a very sad time because Helen had gone off the rails and wasn't taking care of herself, her home was a shithole and worst of all, she was neglecting the children. Brandon was only a baby then and he'd often arrive at ours with a piss-sodden nappy on that was so heavy, it would be hanging down by his knees, poor little mite. All the kids had dirty clothes on and were always put straight into our bath as soon as they got there to have a proper good wash. They ate like starved wildebeests, so they obviously hadn't been eating well either. I fell out with Helen; not because I had sided with Nick, nor due to her affairs but solely because of how she was treating those beautiful kids. I didn't approve and I had told her so.

My Mum always thought the world of Helen and would often say 'She is a good egg but should never have had children'. She would then go into her speech about how totally wrong it is that every woman feels obligated to have children and how she would stay childless if she could live her life over again. I thought it was great, and rather amusing, that my own Mum felt that it was okay to have her say on the matter, even in front of her two daughters; it used to upset my sister a bit though. She is a true Earth Mother, my sister, and believes that a life without having kids is simply a waste of time. If she had been infertile, she would have gone to bits. I tend to think more like my Mum on that particular subject; having children shouldn't be the be-all and end-all. Don't get me wrong, if that's what floats ya boat, great, and if everyone felt the same as me and my Mum the human race would become extinct but life can still be wonderful without becoming a parent and I personally feel like I managed to dodge a bullet when I have listened to many people breaking their hearts over their kids.

Andy always wanted to have children, but I wasn't that bothered. However, the longer we were married, the less he wanted to have them with me, as things went from bad to worse. We did have a funny old relationship really and we had come from such different families. My family were clean, hardworking, homeowners, family orientated, always welcoming and respectable and his were not! I know that sounds a bit harsh, but it's bloody true I tell ya. Honest to God, why I carried on going out with him after he first took me to meet his parents, I will never know. I ain't being horrible right, but they were proper rough. 'Low-life' is a common term used in my neck of the woods and they fitted that terminology perfectly. They had two cats, called Willy and Pussy, no lie, and they were allowed up on the worktops in the kitchen, which was where I first saw one of them, I think it was Willy. He was happily nibbling at the roast chicken that was just about to be hacked up for my dinner, for fuck's sake!!! What I should have done was tell them about my cat allergy, made my apologies and got the hell out of there but no, I discreetly popped an antihistamine and cracked on with it and let the horror continue. Silly Jackie! His Mum, Jean, greeted us and said that I could call her 'Mum' if I wanted to; 'I shouldn't think so sweed'art, not in this lifetime'.

She was a very attractive woman, nice, albeit brassy hair with a full but shapely figure. She modelled herself on Marilyn Monroe she later told me; 'yeah, whatever Love'. She was dressed well, a bit tarty but fair play, she made all her own clothes. She was a dressmaker, like my Mum, but explained that she could never get a job doing it because it would affect their benefits; nice. The Dad didn't want to work, and he'd told her when they'd met, twenty-five years earlier, that he'd never marry her. If he did, he'd have to stop claiming off the dole and that was out of the question. He wasn't ill, just lazy but had managed to get invalidity benefits like, forever. He had told her that she could move in with him though and get money from the state by claiming to be his carer, which she did. He even let her have two kids by him, but a wedding was never going to happen, how sweet, true love that is!

When Jean led us into their sitting room there he was, Kenny, my future father-in-law, sat on the knackered, dirty old sofa in front of the TV. He didn't even look at me, just a horrible grunt came out of his gob and he gave a slight nod of his head. What an ignorant pig that man was; unless he was pissed and then he was all over me, vile creature. His hair was stuck to his head and in desperate need of a wash, like the rest of him, clothes included. Apparently, he'd made an effort for my visit because he usually sat there in just his pants; charmed I'm sure. Jean was obviously nervous, bless her, and was talking too much, too quickly, too high pitched and way too loud. She was a kind soul, not that bright and had just fallen into the strange life she was in. She could have done much better for herself, poor cow. My dinner was presented to me on an old tray and plonked onto my lap. Knives and forks, none of which matched I clocked, along with the salt and pepper were on the dirty coffee table in front of me. As I shuffled forward on the broken sofa, tray on my lap, my arse was almost touching the floor due to the lack of springs in it, my left knee went much higher than my right making my entire dinner slide onto the already dirty carpet. Why the fuck I didn't just think 'Result' and go without dinner, is beyond me. Instead, due to my good upbringing and impeccable manners, I used my hands to scoop the dinner back onto my plate and tucked in, making sounds of joy and appreciation as I ate. Whilst eating that dinner, I must have pulled at least twenty cat hairs out of my mouth and wiped them onto the sofa and felt relieved that nobody caught me doing it. Jean was what she was, but I didn't want to embarrass her by proving how much her carpet needed hoovering. I felt incredibly sick for days afterwards and cringed every time I relived the moment when I ate that chicken and cat hair roast!

Andy had issues regarding sex, due to his parents, it's safe to say. They were heavy drinkers and were quite famous in the local pub but not in a good way. Kenny would sit at the end of the bar, pint of Special Brew in hand trying to look all mean and moody, while Jean would swan about believing that everyone was thinking how much she reminded them of Marilyn Monroe. After their regular pub sessions, they would stagger home, usually with a couple of cans they had purchased for the journey and then fall into bed and have loud sex. One night when I was there, they must have got a bit frisky on their way home from the pub because when they got in, Jean's hair was all over the place and they both had grass stains on their knees; that conjured up a very nasty scene in my head. Andy and his sister, Jane, often had to endure listening to the 'goings on' in their Mum and Dad's bedroom. Jean was a screamer by the sounds of it and that isn't good, especially with your kids are in the rooms next door. Jane, who was five years younger than Andy, used to get into her big brother's bed when she was little because she was frightened; she thought that Daddy was hurting Mummy, shocking! Consequently, Andy never really liked doing it. Nick and I used to regularly tease him about his lack of sex drive, but he'd just laugh and wasn't the slightest bit embarrassed about it. He genuinely believed that he was normal and that we were just sex mad. Nick even got Helen to buy Andy the Ann Summers 'Sex Maniacs Diary' one Christmas. He loved it, he thought it was well funny and even used the bloody thing to plan his nonsexual weeks. He thought that reading the 'Sunday Sport' newspaper to get him going, rolling on top of me, bouncing about for a while, then rolling off was him doing his bit and that was my lot until the following Sunday. About a year into our marriage they started to publish a 'Wednesday Sport'. I thought 'Oh hello, result, twice a week from now on' but alas, no chance. I once suggested that perhaps it would make a change if I got on top of him. He stopped what he was doing, looked at me as though I was a pervert and stormed off downstairs. Helen used to agree that once a week was enough, but Nick and I thought differently.

My marriage to Andy didn't end because of his family or the lack of sex but because of something much more dramatic. We'd been together just over five years and, although I knew deep down that things were not going well, I was still shocked and heartbroken when he got home from work one night and told me that he was leaving me. He said that he was no longer able to cope with my nagging and with me putting him and his family down all the time. Also, the pressure of having a mortgage and bills to pay was stressing him out to the point that he was having to get pissed, way too often, to handle it. He had put on a lot of weight, which he hated, due to his drinking himself into oblivion a few times a week; I used to moan at him about that too!

I dealt with all financial matters and was having to work full time in Top Man and two evenings a week behind a bar in a local night club to be able to cover the bills and to save a bit for holidays and home improvements and boy, did I go on about it. In hindsight, that must have made him feel so inadequate. He used to hand me his wage packet every Friday evening. It was a small brown envelope containing cash and his wage slip and it was always stapled in the middle. One Friday I noticed that the staple had been removed, along with the wage slip when he gave it to me. I was so angry and went on and on asking him to explain to me why he had taken the wage slip out and, I assumed, some of the money. He said repeatedly that he didn't want to tell me because it was a surprise. I really lost it then, I hate surprises and didn't cotton on that it was my birthday the following week so he may have wanted to buy me something nice. Eventually, when I had got near to hysteria, he told me that he had bought me an eternity ring. I was a proper horrible, nasty bastard to him and made him return it and get the money back. Not nice. On the night that he left me I was devastated and begged him to stay, promising that I would stop making him feel so bad about himself but off he went.

I sold our house and started divorce proceedings. The first solicitor that I went to see had to pass me on to one of his colleagues to deal with my case because, years before, I had met him in a club and we had gone out and had, a very short lived, sexual relationship. His face was a picture when he saw me walk into his office and mine must have been too. You don't expect to be reacquainted with an ex-lover when you are filing for a divorce! We did have a good old chat and reminisce before I moved to another office though; it was good to see him but I did feel slightly embarrassed that since I had seen him last, he had qualified as a solicitor and all I had managed to do was get married and separated.

The divorce was almost finalised when, late one night, I got a knock on the door and there was Andy. I had gone backpacking for several months when we'd first separated but I was now back and living in my new little one bedroom house in Basildon, that I had bought a few weeks earlier. I invited him in, we had a long talk and started dating. After a couple of months, it was going well, so we decided to stop the divorce and give us another go. I sold my house and together we bought another one; the three bedroom house, that he ended up leaving five months later!

It was a Saturday night when he left for good. Nick was living with us by then but was out, he was spending the weekend with the kids at Helen's, when Andy proper went on the turn. We weren't even arguing when he suddenly got all aggressive, verbally and physically. What a shock that was! He was pissed but even with a drink in him he was normally so placid; boringly quiet to be truthful. We did now have a very big mortgage, the interest rates had gone ridiculously high and although I was still in control of our money and was not as horrible as I used to be, he must of been feeling the pressure and he just snapped, he lost it big time; the worm turned. I was standing on a foot stool cleaning the kitchen light, yes, I know how to enjoy myself on a Saturday night! He started shouting at me for no reason and then proceeded to kick the stool from under me, sending me crashing towards the hard floor. That obviously wasn't quite enough to relieve his anger, so he kicked and punched me several times for good measure, cracking two of my ribs and breaking my nose. Nice. As I lay there in a pool of my own blood, just seconds after the attack, we heard the front door slam. It was Nick who had seen what had happened through the glass kitchen door as he pulled up outside the house. Helen had got home unexpectedly early after her plans had gone wrong, they'd had an argument so, thankfully, he'd come back to the house. He told Andy to get out and then called an ambulance which turned up with the police.

Even though Andy was drunk when he did what he did and his actions were totally out of character, they were, nevertheless, unacceptable, so he had to go for good. My Mum used to say that Andy came into our lives, stayed for a few years, then left, and nobody really noticed. Terrible thing to say, but she had a point. I wanted to divorce Andy, but I couldn't face going to court so I asked Nick to do me a massive favour and say that we had committed adultery. I had a fucking cheek really because we had never slept together at that point. He did it though, just to help me get a quick and uncomplicated divorce, bless him.

When Andy went, that left just Nick and I living in the house. Both sad, both lonely and deprived of our weekly sex sessions. It was only a matter of time before we got it together. I loved being that close to Nick. I had waited a long time and it was better than I had ever imagined. Of course, Nick being Nick, didn't feel quite the same. After the deed had been done, he looked, what I thought was lovingly into my eyes, and said 'Will I still have to pay rent?'. I was right back at him and replied, 'Oh yes, it'll be double now!'. Not quite the ending to our first time that I'd imagined, cheeky bugger. Things changed a lot from that day on. I insisted that the children came to 'our' house every weekend, so he would no longer have to witness an often-drunk Helen return from her nights out. I loved it and we used to proper spoil the kids. We'd take them for days out, play games with them at home and generally make sure that they enjoyed their time with us. Visiting Southend-on-Sea was a favourite of ours and we even used to let them go on the fairground rides, if we had the money. If we were skint, the kids used to be more than happy just playing around on the beach. They were always very well behaved, so full of fun and they really appreciated anything that we done with them. I'd never really wanted to have children, but I thoroughly enjoyed playing 'step-mum' and I must say, I was pretty good at it; probably because I loved the kids like they were my own. They were, and still are, really great kids, all wonderful in their own way and a real credit to both of their parents. That was one of the happiest times of my life and I never wanted it to end but I knew that Nick didn't love me in the same way that I loved him, so I just made the most of it while it lasted.

That summer Debbie, a girl I worked with, suggested that the two of us go on holiday together to Faliraki in Greece for two weeks. I was a bit shocked because I barely knew her, and didn't like her all that much either, but she was very insistent, so I agreed. She worked for Top Shop and I worked on the floor above her store, for Top Man. We had nothing in common and she was the total opposite to geeky old me; she was one of the 'cool lot' that used to drink in the trendy pub called The Pitsea Bull. I hated that pub because it was full of posers, all bragging about how much money they had and were always crapping on about their flash and expensive cars, that were parked up outside. Quite frankly, they all used to bore the shit out of me. I never have, and never will enjoy the company of people that are false. They all talked a load of 'bull', so it was no wonder that they had made 'The Bull' their drinking hole! I much prefer people that are down-to-earth, say it as it is and if they are a bit crazy too, better still, even more entertaining.

The only two conversations that I'd ever had with Debbie up until the holiday invite, were literally years before when she'd approached me at work and asked what the symptoms of my husband's inner ear infection were, that she'd heard he was suffering from. I told her all about it and then asked why she wanted to know. She said that her Mum had also been having dizzy spells and was acting a bit odd. Several weeks later, when Andy had fully recovered, I bumped into Debbie on the stairs that joined our two stores, so I asked her how her Mum was; she looked at me with a blank expression on her face and said 'Dead.' It's not often that I'm lost for words but fuck me, I was then. Before I offered her my condolences, I asked how her Mum had died and she replied, 'Brain tumour, she was forty-two' and walked off. I actually would have liked to of given her a hug and told her how sad I was for her and her family's loss, but she'd gone.

It was months later when our paths crossed again. This time we had both gone to the back door of our shop to get a delivery in. The week before I had been promoted and had gone out and bought myself a very formal suit. There was absolutely no need for me to have this dramatic change of image, I could have continued to wear the casual stuff that I'd always chucked on, but I had taken my promotion quite seriously. I knew my staff were taking the piss out of me, but I didn't care. I liked my new style, it made me feel all managerial and that. Obviously, I can now see that I was a bit pathetic, but it seemed okay at the time. I had got many deliveries in but never with Debbie and I was feeling a bit nervous because she used to scare the shit out of me to be honest. She was a tiny little thing but was a very strict manager and most of her staff felt the same way as me about her. I unbolted the big double doors to let the delivery driver in and soon discovered that some idiot had decided to stack a load of wood up against them, on the outside. The second that the bolt came off, the doors came towards me at high-speed and so did all the heavy wood. I was pushed onto my back as the full force of the wood hit me and all I could hear was Debbie laughing her head off. It must have looked funny because the only part of me that was on show, was my startled looking face. Debbie and the delivery man removed the wood and helped me up but then Debbie lost it again. She was laughing so much that she couldn't even speak. She'd spotted that one of the many nails in the wood had ripped my lovely new suit beyond repair. Oh well, that put an instant stop to my 'power-dressing' days!

The night before the holiday, Debbie came around to my house and asked if she could see what I had packed. She looked mortified when I showed her and went on to take almost every item out of my case and then replaced it with some of her clothes for me to wear. I was getting frightened again and she was the 'manager' of Top Shop and I was just the 'deputy' of Top Man; so, I let her do what she had to do. She informed me that she thought I had a great slim body since splitting up with Andy, but

I was still dressing like a fat bird and that she would feel embarrassed walking around with me if I wore my usual clothing. She totally had a point. Perhaps it was time for a change of image. I was only twenty-five, almost twenty-six, so sod it, why the hell not and off we went to Greece.

What a fantastic holiday that was. Debbie had pre-warned me that if I had sex with anyone, she would disown me and I would have to spend the rest of the holiday without her; fair enough, sort of. When we arrived in Greece, I wore my first ever Lycra dress, made my hair big via vigorous backcombing and lots of hairspray and even put some make-up on. I looked so different, in a good way, and I was liking this new look. I drew the line when Debbie suggested high heels because I tend to walk like I've shit myself if I wear anything other than flats. That night changed my life; it made me open my eyes and realise that I was not making the most of my youth. I'd got myself stuck in a rut and was dressing, talking and acting like an old bird. I loved the

90's dance music. I'd never really listened to it before that night and I instantly knew that my usual Radio 2, Neil Diamond, Barbra Streisand and Elkie Brooks could fuck right off, but not Donny Osmond, never my Donny! When I first walked into a Faliraki club they were playing 'My love has got no money, he's got his trumberlease'. 'What the fuck's a trumberlease?' I thought; 'who gives a shit, let's dance!'. Of course, it isn't trumberlease it's 'strong beliefs' but yeah, whatever! I looked at the way the other occupants of the packed dance floor were moving and thought 'I can do that'. I soon had my arms above my head punching the air, eyes closed and stomping my feet and dancing like nobody was watching, which they probably weren't because the eye shutting thing seemed quite popular.

Debbie went to the bar and bought us both a shot, a Burning B52 it was called, due to the fact that it was actually on fire I assumed. I'd never done a shot before and I liked the way it made me feel. It was whilst drinking my first shot that I realised that I had a moustache because it ignited, as did the nose hair, that I also never knew that I had until that point. Debbie said that she'd been wanting to mention my facial hair problem for some time but had never got around to it. Oh well, no need to tell me now, I was fully aware of it. After a couple more shots were downed, through a straw to avoid the flames, we were back on the dance floor. We even sat on the floor when they played 'Sit Down' by James. In the past I had always point blank refused to sit on a germ-ridden, dirty dance floor when 'Oops upside ya head' had been played but things were different now. I felt sexy and gorgeous and let all my inhibitions go. All the male attention we were getting was making me wanna burst with confidence. When the music, and probably the shots, had really got to me I danced over to one of the giant speakers, thinking I looked the bollocks, closed my eyes and proper went for it. I probably looked like a right twat but then so did everyone else, so what the hell.

Several nights into the holiday we met a group of lads from Wembley. There were twelve of them and I had gotten so cock-sure of myself that I truly believed that they all fancied me. The one that I went for, was Lenny. He was a handsome bugger and at twenty years old, the youngest of the group; dirty old bitch or what! We spent the rest of the holiday with our Wembley boys, they were great company and a proper good laugh. They even made my cool friend Debbie dance to 'The Music Man'. I was so shocked to see her let her inhibitions go and act like me, a geek or I should say 'ex' geek now! There she was up on the bar singing 'pi-a-pi-a pi-ano, pi-ano, pi-ano' and 'oompa-oompa-oompa-pa' doing the actions and everything! Good for her! I realised at that moment that this holiday was also going to be a life-changer for her too. Who wants to be cool, or a geek, all of the time, mix it up a bit I say, do whatever you want to do, fuck what anybody else thinks of you, just enjoy yourself and be happy. Obviously, the no-sex rule was still on, but it was the last night of the holiday so, I broke the rules, a few times if I remember rightly. I thought that I could show Lenny a thing or two in the bedroom. I was six years older than him and a divorcee, he needed to brace himself! I couldn't have been more wrong. He was so passionate and full of energy that I didn't know what had hit me. He lived so far away from Basildon so I knew I would have to make the most of our time together because I'd never see him again. Consequently, we had the wildest, most unselfconscious and adventurous bunk-up(s) that I'd ever had; it was fucking awesome. Lenny and his mates still had a few more nights of their holiday left, so we said our goodbyes that night. The coach was coming to collect me and Debbie very early the following morning, so it was goodbye to Faliraki and goodbye to Lenny all within a few hours. I was a bit sad but okay because I knew that I would never be the same again after this holiday and was looking forward, and not back. As we boarded the coach the silence was broken by the sound of 'I've had the Time of My Life' from the Dirty Dancing film playing very loudly. When we looked, there was Lenny with a big stereo on his shoulder and grinning like a Cheshire Cat. He had come to wave us off; I was chuffed to bits. I got off the coach and we had one last big cuddle, whilst the people watching all said 'bless' a lot. I got back on the coach and off to the airport we went.

Was I thinking about Nick when I launched into this holiday romance? Well no, because a couple of weeks before I went on holiday, Nick told me that he had met a girl, liked her and was going to take her on a date. He had a new best friend, Barry; little bloke Del had blown Nick out one too many times, probably because he had realised that Nick was too tall and good-looking to be his friend anymore. Nick had met Barry's sister, Dawn, on a night out and they had hit it off. I was beyond gutted because I had been putting off suggesting to Nick that we become an official item and wanted the kids to come live with us permanently. I liked my job, but I would have happily of given it up to become a full-time step-mum. Not only was I completely and utterly in love with him, but I loved the kids too. Helen wasn't taking care of the children, so I wanted us to go for custody of them. I had put it off for too long and missed the boat! I had a feeling that Nick and Dawn were gonna make a go of it and I was right. The timing of the holiday turned out to be perfect.

Within a week of Lenny getting home from his holiday, he managed to get my landline number and phoned me. He said he'd love to see me again, so I invited him to Basildon the following weekend. The night before he arrived, I lay awake listening to Nick and Dawn having a bit of slap and tickle; I hated it and I admit, I was jealous. I didn't want to slap or tickle Dawn you understand; my lesbian phase didn't come until many years later. It was so good to see Lenny again. We had an excellent weekend, but he just wasn't Nick.

That was it now, after Lenny had gone home I decided it was now or never, I was going to sit Nick down and tell him how much I loved him and hit him with my plan about us making a proper go of it. When he got home from work on that Monday night, like planned, I sat him down and for some reason completely different words came spewing out of my stupid gob. I told him that I was selling the house and so he would have to find somewhere else to live but that there was no rush. Seriously, where the fuck did that come from?!! I had never considered selling the house, it was in negative equity for a start, as most homes were in the early 1990's. Selling wasn't an option. If I had sold it then I wouldn't have been able to pay my mortgage off. A moment of pure madness. I believe that regret is a wasted emotion and try never to regret anything that I do or say, but that was a close one. Nick and Dawn later had two beautiful daughters together, Abigail and Ellie; so, you see, everything does happen for a reason. If I had made my planned speech, perhaps he would have agreed and then those two lovelies, who are equally as amazing as Nick's other five children, may not have been born either.

Chapter 4 Mindy moved in with us, I married Lenny

Lenny and I continued our long-distance relationship. Nick stayed living at the house for many more months, but things got easier with Dawn and Lenny being there a lot and I got another lodger in, Mindy. I informed Nick that I was going to start interviewing people to rent the spare room and he begged me to get a female lodger; preferably with big boobies, for an extra bit of eye candy for him. I was sat on the sofa with Mindy who had popped round to see the room, when in walked Nick. He politely said 'Hello' and then proceeded to stand behind her doing a dramatic, over-the-top throat cutting action. She really did not look like what he had been hoping for. The poor girl had a wonky eye, 'one eye looking at ya and one looking for ya' and a dodgy hip which made her walk like she should be saying 'times is 'ard'. She was ridiculously pear-shaped, the end of her nose was almost touching her right cheek as though her face was permanently squashed up against a window, she shouted when she spoke and had a speech impediment to boot, a right fucking state in other words. She was only in her early twenties but looked well in her thirties. I knew straight away that she wasn't wired up properly, but I felt so sorry for her and I offered her the room on a three month trial basis. Nick's reaction was priceless; he looked so shocked and actually went foetal on the kitchen floor. Nick later said that he was sure that I had invited her into our home to speed up his departure; perhaps I did, but it was done subconsciously if that was the case.

What a bleedin' nightmare Mindy turned out to be. I knew she wasn't going to be the easiest of house guests, but I never imagined how much trouble one person could make. She really was a complete and utter fucking loony tune, and some and the few months that she lived with us were eventful, to say the least. As well as working full-time at Top Man, now in the Southend branch, I worked a few evenings during the week too as an Ann Summers party organiser, which I enjoyed lots. Although I do say so myself, I was excellent at it and earned shitloads of extra cash and I met some funny fuckers at the many parties that I did over the years. Women are funny creatures really; they act so very differently when there are no blokes about to impress or feel protective over. The stories that I used to hear, about their sex lives mainly, sometimes actually shocked me and that takes some doing. I am quite loud and a bit outspoken, but nothing compared to some of the old sorts that I came across at these parties. One woman, a nurse, told a wonderful story about the day she missed the bus, on purpose. She explained that to help her get through her stressful and hard-working day, she would always pop 'duo balls' up her noony before she left home to travel to the hospital. Duo balls look very similar to Clackers, the popular toy from the 1970's, but the Ann Summers version have got shorter strings and perhaps not quite as heavy; you wouldn't want them falling out when you were out doing your weekly shop! One morning, the bus pulled up early at the top of her road and she had to break into a jog, so not to miss it. She was a good eighteen stone this woman, so that really took some doing. The old duo balls started jumping about inside her, giving her a nice cheap thrill. The faster she ran, the faster the balls moved so when she got to the bus she said to the driver 'Move on sir, I am jogging to work today'. Dirty cow but fucking funny.

As an Ann Summers party organiser back then, you would start the party by explaining to the group that their orders were all confidential and at the end of the evening they were to fill out their order forms, seal them up and I would send them off to head office who would bag the goods up, send them to me and I would then deliver the well-sealed bags to them a few days after the party. I'm not sure how other organisers worked but I used to get home after the party, rip the confidential orders open, do one mass order and bag the stuff up myself when I got it.

I only ever had one bad Ann Summers party. It was in a Conservative Club that was way too many miles away really, but I had been promised a nice big crowd, so the drive would be worth it. The place was full of rich bitches who done sod all apart from get their hair and nails done whilst their hardworking husbands ploughed the money into the joint bank account (and probably shagged their secretaries at every given opportunity). I earned a good few quid that night but boy, did I suffer for it. Most organisers, like me, always started the demonstration by giving every lady a catalogue. Then, from my giant bag, I would start removing the stuff like the underwear, nighties etc. and make the customers look at the items in their catalogues as I done this. That way, basically I was forcing them to look at every item available; it ups the sales you see. This is normally the ice breaker, the wine starts flowing, the tongues start to loosen, and the fun begins. That was not the case on this shit night, however. They all started criticising the quality of the underwear, saying that you could get much nicer things in much better fabric from John Lewis and Marks & Spencer, not a good start. The next stage of the proceedings is a game or two. I was never one to do the sort of games that involved them getting out of their seats, like the one where everyone has to pass a cock shaped balloon

96

round, using only their knees or pinning the knob on the man, an adult version of pinning the tail on the donkey because I used to feel the pain of the less outgoing ladies in the room when they got embarrassed having to do silly things. My favourite was the alphabet game. We all remained seated and I would simply say a letter of the alphabet. The first person to shout out a body part beginning with that letter would be given a playing card, an Ann Summers playing card of course, which had hardcore porn on, obviously. The one with the most cards at the end of the game would get a prize, something classy like a pair of crotchless drawers, a small pretend willy or a bra that ya nips poked out of. I always started with the letter 'B' because it was an easy one. Lots of choices like boobs, balls or bollocks followed by 'P' for prick, pussy or penis for the less crude ladies, you get the idea. My last letter was always 'C' to see if anyone was brave enough to say the ultimate 'C' word! They would get a bonus card if they said it. That night was a corker, my game was a total disaster. I got 'finger', no chance of a fanny or flange. Then someone proudly shouted 'toe', tits and testes weren't getting a look in, but the best one had to be 'cornea'. Seriously, oh fuck off, what sort of lives were these bints living?! The final part of my demonstration, hidden right at the bottom of my bag, were the toys. Some big, some small, some black, some pink but all with a very powerful vibrating action! I hated the new one that had just came out; it was called the 'Rampant Rabbit'. The worst name ever for me because I am unable to pronounce my R's properly. I have a bit of the Jonathan Ross going on, but that always caused a laugh but of course, not tonight!!!!

They made me feel like a Basildon low-life and the pits of the earth who had come to their beloved 'Con Club' to try to entertain them by showing them cheap underwear, play silly games and now showing them disgusting sex toys. The toys are always switched on first, before getting passed around the room. This is normally the funniest part of the evening because of the different reactions of the customers. This stuck-up lot were throwing them from one person to the next, as though they were on fire or had been up my noony before I had arrived at the party, fucking cheek. When I finally got home, feeling pretty shit to be honest, I opened their orders. I could not believe it; I'd hardly sold any underwear, but I had never ever sold so many toys in one night before. They'd really gone for it and the best seller of the night was the Adonis; the biggest vibrator we sold with the biggest girth and I also sold shitloads of love oil, which one would assume they needed to get the toys up there tight arses. Just goes to show, you should never judge a book by its cover eh! It always used to equally amaze me when you'd get a right old foul mouthed, rough as arseholes women at a party and nine times out of ten, they would only order underwear and they were just giving it large with the toys, acting like they loved them just to amuse their friends. It's a funny old world.

Repacking your bag correctly at the end of each party is a very important part of being a successful party organiser. You need to be ready for the next party, so you can just open your bag and there would be the first item, right at the top, which would be shown on page one of my ladies' catalogues. Mindy had only moved in a few days before, when I went off to do my next party. When I arrived at my customers house, I opened my bag and to my horror, the bag had been all muddled up. Someone had obviously been into the bag and had a good old rummage through it. I instantly thought of Nick; perhaps he'd had a pervy moment? Shame on me, I knew that he would never go through my stuff without telling me. This happened again at my next couple of parties, so I asked Mindy if she had touched my work bag; she went all red and denied it but from that day on, my bag was never messed up again, strange that innit?!

On the rare occasion that I got a bit of time to relax, I would go foetal on the nice big comfy chair that was nearest the CD player in our lounge. Then, I'd pop one of my favourite albums on and have a little read, heaven. One night I got home from work a bit early, only to find Mindy, or 'Mad Mindy' as we now called her, sat foetal in my chair, just like I would, with Otis Reading blasting away, my book in her hand and get this, she had one of my dresses on! Very calmly, I explained to her that I was unhappy with her wearing my clothes, especially without at least asking my permission first. I didn't even mention all the other bollocks coz, quite frankly, I was a bit scared. She started crying and said that she hated herself and wanted to be me; now I was shitting myself! My initial reaction was to call her a crazy bitch and tell her to get the fuck out of my house, but I still felt sorry for her because she was obviously mental. So instead I suggested she joined some sort of club (yeah right, for nutty freaks) or could she not ask any of her work friends from Tesco's to go to the cinema with her (what, to see 'Single White Female'?) or even to put a lonely hearts ad in the local newspaper to get a boyfriend (like 'Fred West' you psycho).

Lenny and I went away that weekend and I told him my latest Mad Mindy story, as ever, he thought it was hysterical. Lenny dropped me back home after our nice break, late on the Sunday night and then he headed back home to Wembley. The following morning, I was just about to get into my car to go to work, when the lovely old couple who lived next door to us, called me over to them. They said that they felt a bit awkward telling me, as though they were telling tales, but they thought I should know. Apparently, while Lenny and I were away, Mad Mindy spent a lot of time sitting in my car with the radio on and just staring into space. I thanked them for letting me know and laughed to myself when they said, 'We don't think Mindy is all the ticket', no shit Sherlock. I got into my car and, no surprise, it wouldn't start; the battery was as flat as a witch's tit, nice one Mindy!

We all have a breaking point and regarding Mad Mindy, Nick's was when he got home from work one night and found her laying on his bed looking at one of his porno mags; she was fully clothed at least. I had to laugh at that one, mainly because of Nick's reaction. He was proper upset and said that his porn collection would never be the same again! The final straw for me was when Nick told me that all the pound coins had disappeared from the penny jar that he kept in his room. We knew it was her but wanted to be 100% sure before we kicked her out. We put another five pound coins in the jar and shook it up a bit. Time would tell.

Before she managed to fall into our trap however, we had the Christmas tree incident. It was early December, so I rearranged the furniture in the lounge, leaving a big empty space in one corner. Bang in the middle of the space, I left a note that read 'Nick, please get back into ya Transit Van and go get us a big old Christmas tree, Love Jackie xx'. I put a tenner next to the note, you could get a beauty for ten pounds then, and I went out. When I returned home, there was an amazing Christmas tree in the lounge and Nick with a face like a smacked arse. He did his nut at me, saying that he didn't mind going to get the tree but thought I was bang out of order making him pay for it. That was it then; the fucking nutcase 'was' a thief. I was so angry but hurt too. She had told me, just days before, how much she liked living with us. We often had parties, which she'd absolutely love and not only had Nick and I made her feel welcome and like one of the gang but both of our families and all of our friends had done so too. I was seriously pissed off. She denied it at first, saying that she had sucked the tenner up the hoover. No problem then, let's get the hoover and empty the bag out, but she said she had already done that and the ten pound note was all shredded up, so then she'd walked the dustbin sack to Pitsea tip; a four mile round journey, yeah right! Silly girl, she obviously thought that I was as thick as her. Big mistake! I told Mindy to phone her equally as odd sister and tell her to come and collect her and her stuff within the hour. Good riddance, you ungrateful little cunt!!!

Now, you will have probably noticed that I just used the word 'cunt'. Most of the people that I've come across in my life, tend to look like they have just had acid thrown into their faces when they hear that word. I'm sorry but I think it can sometimes be the 'only' suitable word in the English language, in certain circumstances. To finalise the Mad Mindy eviction story, being one of these times. I don't like hearing it when it's just dropped into a conversation willy-nilly, for no apparent reason but not because I hate the word, quite the opposite. I think it's an excellent and very powerful word and should be respected, thus, only using it when the time is right. I have worked as a barmaid in many places over the years, normally as a second job to boost my income. One night, whilst I was working behind the bar in a local working man's club, I handed a female customer her change and said, 'Thank you my love' and went on to serve the next customer. She grabbed my arm and said, 'Don't you ever call me love again, I am not your love and never will be!'. Again, this is one of those special moments when that wonderful word is the only suitable one to use. I replied to her nasty comment by asking her, 'What would you like me to call you? Cunt?'. See what I'm saying, it can be a brilliant word.

Lenny was still living with his parents, but we spent most weekends at my house, which was still not up for sale by the way! Sometimes, during the week, we would talk on the phone and realise how much we were missing each other. He'd get in his car and drive the fifty-two miles from Wembley, sometimes late at night, just for a cuddle. He would then have to leave me at silly o'clock in the morning to go back home and then to work. Young love eh! My family loved Lenny, especially my two eldest nieces, Scarlet, then aged eight and six-year-old Rosie. My sister, Chrissie, also had Georgia, who had just turned one and baby Gracie, who had only just arrived. Over the years, I have been lucky to have had so many excellent people cross my path, family, friends, husbands and lovers. Some came and fucked off, but lots have stayed. I truly love each and every one of them, but then, in a league of their own, I have got my four nieces, and now their kids too! My sister having children was the best thing to ever happen to me, not her obviously, because it's all about me! My beautiful nieces and their children are simply my world, my reason for being here. They are my friends and the only people that I would actually die for. I often tell them that they are arsehole lucky that I never bashed out kids of my own because then they would not of got a look in and they would certainly have been written out of my will, that's for sure!

Georgia and Gracie were totally unaware that their new Uncle Lenny was the most handsome, albeit, pretty-boy ever, but Scarlet and Rosie could see it. He was their idol and pin-up boy and they had loads of photos of him, with me cut out, on their bedroom wall. Not only was he very pleasing on the eye, but he could sing and used to entertain them on his own personal karaoke machine. He was also a martial arts champion and they used to be star-struck when he'd put on his white karate gear and do demonstrations for them. He was young, good-looking, fit and talented but, when I look back, so unbelievably effeminate. The night before I married him, one of my friends, Lauren, phoned me and begged me not to go through with the wedding because she was certain that Lenny, like Eddie and Charlie, my first two lovers, was gay! She just couldn't understand why nobody else had ever warned me or how I couldn't see it myself because he was more camp than a row of tents! She also pointed out that no straight man would admit that he loved Donny Osmond as much as I did or feel okay about waxing my moustache once a week or be so bad at DIY or have such limp wrists or dance to Abba the way he did or have such a need to have so many cushions all around the house! I didn't listen to her and I'm glad I didn't because the wedding was perfect, and I do love a good day out me! I needed to have a good one because my first wedding was shit really, mainly due to the fact that I didn't particularly want to get married at the time but just thought that I should, consequently I made no effort at all.

It was in a registry office and there were only twenty of us in attendance, including me and Andy. We had only invited both sets of parents, both of our sisters with their partners, my old Nan and eight of our friends; including Helen and Nick of course. I also had Scarlet there, she was my only niece then and the cutest two year old ever. She was my bridesmaid and looked so gorgeous in her little pink Cinderella dress that my Mum had made for her, big bless. I wore a terrible, old fashioned even then, white suit and hat from Etam, cheap plastic shoes that were very high so I couldn't walk properly. I weighed more than Andy and emphasised that fact by wearing a nasty old silky pink blouse that was way too small for me; just to nicely complete the awful outfit. To top it all, I was forever eating fried food and cakes, that had not only made me proper fat but had also given me a giant zit on my chin that I'd had a good old pick at before the wedding so, on the day, it looked like a giant cornflake stuck to my face; beautiful. We had a few photographs taken outside the registry office after the ten minute service that was conducted by a bloke with an horrific speech impediment that made him spit all over anyone that was close to him and then we all went back to my Mum and Dad's, where the one tiered wedding cake and small buffet were. A few more photos were taken with the cake and then everyone went home. That evening we had booked a table at the local carvery, that had the smallest dance floor you have ever seen and treated our guests to a dinner and a few drinks. My Mum had to tell Helen and Nick off that night because they both had smacked-arse faces on. They had the hump because I had asked them not to bring baby Nick to the registry office. He was only three months old and I was worried that he might cry all the way through the service. I now think that I was out of order for not wanting him there, but at the time I didn't think it was a big deal. They were proper pissed off about it but had never told me, instead they just sat at the dinner table silently sulking. After my Mum pulled them up about their attitude, we cleared the air and cracked on. Wow, that was a wedding to forget if ever there was one!

Lenny and I however, we did our wedding in style; like only a possible closet gay man and a drama queen could do. My Mum looked lovely in her outfit. It was a dress, jacket and a great big hat that matched my six bridesmaids' colours perfectly. I had six bridesmaids, aged between two and fourteen, they all wore Cinderella dresses, each one in a different shade of pastel. I think they call it a rainbow wedding; they looked breathtakingly beautiful and seriously cute. Prior to the wedding day, I had told Lenny that I was going to wear a nice black evening gown and my Doc Martin boots but when me and my Dad arrived at the church, in a chauffeur-driven Mercedes, I got out of the car in my tight-fitting, long, cream satin wedding dress. I was going through a slim phase, I had my hair and make-up done by a professional and, although I do say so myself, I looked the bollocks. Helen had made all the flowers for the wedding; mine and the bridesmaid's bouquets and the table decorations, they were perfect. Helen attended the wedding with her new partner, Richard and the four children. Nick came with Dawn, now pregnant with their first child. This was the second time Helen and Nick had seen me get married, it still seemed odd that this time they were both with their new partners. It's funny how much can change in between my wedding days!

Our first dance as newlyweds had to be 'I've had the Time of My Life' which had been 'our tune' ever since he came to wave me goodbye in Faliraki with it playing on his stereo. We danced to it at the wedding the best we ever had, it was brill and I've got the video to prove it. Nick approached me that night and said that he thought it was odd that, in the early 1990's, I had told him that I was gonna sell the house and yet it was now the mid 1990's and I was still living in it! I just laughed and shrugged it off. Did he realise then, that I'd loved him with all of my heart when I'd asked him to leave? I've asked him since, but he won't comment. Nick sometimes comes across as a Jack the Lad and ain't keen on deep, meaningful chats, but I know he is a much deeper thinker than he lets on.

It was such a great wedding, with lots of memorable moments. During the day, whilst we were eating the after-ceremony dinner, Nick's eldest daughter, Chloe, then eight years old, approached the top table and told me that she thought I looked like a beautiful princess. I thanked her and said, 'One day, I will be at your wedding and you will also look like a beautiful princess'. She frowned, looked a bit confused and said, 'But you will be dead by then Jackie'. Everyone heard her adorable comment and burst out laughing. Chloe has been with her partner for seventeen years now, they have four wonderful children, but she's still not married. She'd better get her finger out and marry her Danny soon or her premonition may well be right!

Lenny and I got married in the same year that the film 'Four Weddings and a Funeral' was released and my Dad, in true LBS fashion, spent the whole night swerving about repeating his new favourite line 'I've only got two daughters and this is the fourth wedding between them, it's like that new film innit, Four Weddings.....it will be my bleedin' funeral next!'

Many of Lenny's friends were Asian or black, so my Dad thought it'd be funny to say to one of the black lads 'Nice tan, you been away?'. Now, he got a laugh from that line see, so he then spent the next hour looking for any people of colour so he could repeat his new, what he thought was a classic line, to each and every one of them. Thankfully, nobody took offence to his totally politically in-correctness because they knew he did mean it offensively.

He was a cocky little fucker my Dad, but very likeable and funny; love him. He had some great lines. Whenever he had to propose a toast he would always say, at the end of his normally very long and funny speech, whatever the occasion, 'Raise ya glasses, here's to my wife's husband'. He was a good public speaker and my Mum would be proud of him until he inevitably ended with his famous line. It used to confuse the hell out of people!

Everyone was poised to raise a glass to 'the bride and groom' or to 'the birthday girl' but no, they had to toast 'him'. If he was being introduced to a stranger, it would be a firm handshake followed by him saying, 'It's your pleasure meeting me'. He used lots of Cockney rhyming slang on a daily basis, always referring to his socks as his 'almonds' (almond rocks) and if he was having a shave he'd be having a 'dig' (dig in the grave), his magnificent head of hair, that he was so proud of until his dying day, was his 'Barnet' (Barnet Fair) but the worst one was when he was going for a poo; he'd feel the need to announce to everyone that he was going for a 'pony' (pony and trap – crap). Nice. He was such a happy and sociable bloke and loved being centre of attention but when he got old and ill, not so much so, obviously. His illness used to make him get very tired, so if he had a room full of visitors it used to get to him after a while, so he'd say 'Thanks for going' and that was ya cue to bugger off; at least you knew that you could never outstay your welcome with my Dad!

I didn't have a honeymoon after my first wedding, so I really wanted to this time around. So, Lenny and I went to Great Yarmouth, not very exotic but better than nothing. We stayed in a crappy old bed and breakfast that had not been decorated, or cleaned, since the early 1970's. The hallway smelt musty and had the most hideously lairy and threadbare Axminster carpet ever. In our bedroom, there was a dusty old lampshade that had those tassel things hanging from it and a candlewick quilt on the bed, not the perfect honeymoon suite! The honeymoon had to be done on the cheap you see because we had done most of our money on the wedding. Both sets of parents had chucked a fair amount of money towards the cost, but we had done a free bar, which my Dad had insisted on, so it was a wonderful, but very expensive day out.

On the way back from Great Yarmouth, we went to the Epsom Derby; one of the few race meetings that we hadn't been to before. That was our thing, going to the races, we had travelled all over the country to various race days and had twice been to Paris to attend the Arc de Triomphe race weekends. Neither of us were big gamblers, we just loved the atmosphere and excitement of going to a racetrack. We always got tickets for the posh area too because we both really enjoyed dressing up and sipping champers. My parents came with us once, to the Boxing Day meeting at Kempton Park, and proper enjoyed it. My Mum had never really gambled before, apart from once a year when my Dad used to make us all pick a horse out for the Grand National, but she managed to pick the winning horse in all but one of the races. She was a natural and simply picked the winners because she liked their names. It's a shame but she never went again, because her winning streak pissed my Dad off. He was a keen gambler and often visited the local bookies but that was his first time at an actual race meeting, and he took it very seriously, studying every horse's form, looking at the condition of the track, considering the weather and all that bollocks; he didn't win a single race!

Lenny came to live with me in Basildon about a year before we got married because I had gotten quite ill, had lost shitloads of weight, without the aid of a fat club for once, and was feeling very tired all the time. The doctor sent me for tests, and I was diagnosed with cervical cancer. Thank fuck it was early stages, so the treatment wasn't too bad, and I was cancer-free within a few months. Looking on the bright side, I looked fantastic in my wedding dress thanks to my illness!

On the day of the move, we managed to get both of us into his old Ford Escort and all his stuff. He didn't really have much, his clothes, vinyl collection, a few books and of course, his pride and joy, that fucking karaoke machine! He bloody loved that thing, he would spend most of his free time standing in the corner of the lounge singing away, all serious with his eyes shut and that, cupping the microphone with both hands, glancing at me lovingly every now and again, giving me the odd cheeky wink or a quick, sudden tilt to one side of his head accompanied by a quick jerk of an outstretched arm and pointed finger, fantasising he was doing a concert at Wembley stadium; bless him.

The biggest change for us as newlyweds was when Lenny walked in one night with a tiny puppy. He fitted into the palm of his hand and he was a ball of ginger loveliness. I was pissed off at first because I had been ill and was on long term sick from work. The cancer had come back, in my ovaries this time which was not so easy to get rid of! The treatment was harsh, and I wasn't keen on the fact that I'd have to take care of a puppy or a 'shitting machine' as my Dad called dogs. I instantly made a few rules; the dog would live in the kitchen and garden, never go into the lounge and certainly not upstairs and Lenny would be the shit shoveler. Within twenty-four hours I was referring to myself as 'Mummy' and he had the run of the entire house. Not only was he allowed upstairs, but he used to sleep on our bed. We spoilt him rotten, if ever there was a substitute baby, it was my Basil. I had always mugged off what I called 'dog prats' that used to talk to their dogs like they were human, buying them birthday and Christmas presents and saying ridiculous statements to them in high pitched voices, but that was me now. I did at least make my dog pratness include topical issues by saying, in a high-pitched voice of course, things like 'He's so big, he's Titanic' or 'He's so big, he's Millennium Dome dog.' I had to constantly reassure my 'little' Basil that he was big because he suffered from LDS, little dog syndrome. Basil's mum was a Jack Russell that had escaped one day and came back pregnant. We used to say that she must have been had by a fox because of his ginger fur. Basil wasn't the only new member of our home, we were skint, so we rented out the two spare bedrooms. I was at home, unable to work, so we thought we'd make some money by me becoming a landlady.

First in, was Shane. I have always been good with accents, which is just as well because Shane was from Derry and had the strongest and most wonderful northern Irish accent ever. Poor Lenny truly couldn't understand a word Shane said, I had to translate like he was talking a foreign language. The night Shane moved in he asked if his girlfriend, who lived in London, could stay the night. Obviously, we agreed and met the beautiful, inside and out, Joanne. We just hoped that they wouldn't be too uncomfortable in the single bed, Nick's old bed, in Shane's new bedroom. Joanne was a very well spoken, sweet, well-educated girl and as blonde as her boyfriend was dark, they made a handsome couple. We had a nice evening together, the four of us, and then they said goodnight and went upstairs to bed. Within two minutes it started, the rhythmic banging, steady with not too much force at first but then, after about five minutes, the banging picked up a bit of pace and a sense of urgency kicked in. Lenny and I were downstairs in the lounge watching a bit of telly, but we kept glancing at each other, not knowing what to say and believe you me, that was not normal for us, we could both talk for England. The final minute was priceless, we thought the light on the living room ceiling was gonna come down and Basil started barking in time with every quick-fire bang. Then it stopped, we heard them walking about, the toilet flushed and then we heard footsteps coming down the stairs. Why Lenny and I were embarrassed I just don't know, but we had both proper gelled up and pretended to be engrossed in the TV. Shane walked in, all red and sweaty, no sign of embarrassment at all and said, 'That double blow up bed I just bought was a nightmare to inflate with the foot pump that had come with it'. Classic! A lesson never to jump to conclusions, eh!

Shane had just graduated from Belfast University and was about to start his first job as an engineer for Fords, in nearby Dunton. Joanne, also just out of university, was now a qualified schoolteacher just like our next lodger, Harry, fondly known by the many people that love him, me included, as 'Tall Harry.' He is six foot six, so I feel that this a fitting nickname for, who is now, one of my closest and dearest friends. Harry had started his first job and was teaching in a school a mile or so away from our home. My two eldest nieces attended the school but neither of them were in Harry's class, but obviously they knew him. He'd truly had the worst few months of his life. He had left the university up in the north of England, where he'd had a good old social life, moved down to Basildon and rented a bedsit, unbeknown to him, in one of the roughest areas in our town. He liked the actual bedsit, but his neighbours were all druggy, low-life wrong-uns. He looked underfed, stressed and seemed depressed. He had no friends in Basildon and all his work colleagues were married, so no chance of a single bloke getting a look in there, so he felt very lonely and in desperate need of some company. The final straw for Harry was when some scumbag tossers broke into his bedsit and robbed him. I must say that the bastards took everything that Harry owned, except for his record collection because, let's just say this, it isn't to everybody's liking!

Harry was lower than low when he spotted my ad, neatly written on a postcard in a newsagent's window in Basildon's town centre.

He phoned me, came to see the room, and took it immediately and I am very pleased that he did, and so is he. The room was way too small for a big bloke like Harry really, but the four of us, and Basil of course, got on brilliantly. Lenny, Shane, Harry and I were all very different characters, but it worked. Harry was the final piece of our perfect jigsaw puzzle and when he joined the gang, we all laughed lots and lots. Harry's now very happily married to the amazing Marie and has been for many years. They met at Harry's next teaching job, up in Yorkshire. Harry and Marie are the most special, thoughtful, non-demanding, funny, entertaining and kind friends that I've ever had in my life. Marie often mentions how grateful she is to me for giving Harry a home when he needed it, bless her; it was a pleasure and certainly not a chore.

The ovarian cancer was a proper bastard to get shot of, but I managed it, although it knocked the shit out of me. I was then diagnosed with M.E. (Myalgic Encephalomyelitis). People think

I'm a nutter for saying this, but it really was worse than the two cancers put together, truly! It's like having the worst hangover ever, but it lasts for months and in my case, years. For the first time ever I 'felt' seriously unwell and ridiculously tired. Sometimes I was unable to get out of bed, even to have a wee, and was in so much pain, mentally as well as physically. Throughout all of my illnesses and trust me, there's been a few, I've always managed to get to school or work, still do my swimming that I love and function like an 'almost' normal human being but the M.E. knocked me for six. I would get the occasional good day but then I tended to go mad and do loads of stuff because it felt so wonderful to feel normal again and then the next day it felt like I'd been hit by a fucking bus. I believe that my biggest achievement to date is going to a specialist, taking his advice and managing to continue with my life again, even though I believe that it never truly goes away, you just learn to manage it. I'd like to say that Lenny was very understanding, caring and thoughtful during my ill years but he wasn't. He always tended to live in 'Lenny's world' and never gave much thought as to what was happening in other people's lives. Without my family and friends, I think I would have either gone mad or literally starved to death but whatever, I survived and am a stronger person for it.

Chapter 5 We lost touch, I divorced Lenny

Everybody loved my Lenny; he really was a smashing bloke, full of fun, a great singer and dancer, very slim and fit and an all-round sportsman. As well as doing his karate, he also played football. The group of lads that he was holidaying with when I met him, were the other members of the football team that he played for; The Bluebirds they were called, and they had won a few trophies in the past, so they must have been good football players, I really wouldn't know, I'm not a fan. I have always agreed with the statement 'football is the sport where men pretend to be hurt and rugby is the sport where men pretend not to be'. What a nice bunch of lads they were, we socialised with them lots, parties at my house and many a good do was had in Wembley. It was a sad day when he left that football team, but he'd started to play semi-professional for an Essex team, Benfleet United but the Bluebirds gave him an excellent send-off at the end of his last season with them. At the end-of-season party, they awarded him the Player of the Year trophy, for the third year on the bounce and wonderful things were said about him during the evening's speeches. They all thought the world of him, he was a great character and I know that he is still friends with most of them today.

A local wine bar in Kenton, a couple of miles outside of Wembley, sponsored the football team so we all went there for drinks after the Sunday matches and on numerous other occasions. Many a good drunken night was spent in there I can tell ya. It was run by a nice Asian family, as most businesses are in that neck of the woods. Lenny and I popped in there one mid-week evening because things had started to get a bit awkward at Lenny's house and we just wanted somewhere that we could be on our own and chill. When we walked up to the bar, we were told that we couldn't drink in there that night because it was Diwali. Lenny slapped his forehead, apologised and said he'd forgotten and off we went. I didn't know what the fuck was going on, but he explained to me that once a year, there's a celebration that only people of certain religions can attend. I done my nut because I know for a fact that if, let's say on St George's Day, all pubs owned by British folk said that no non-Brits could enter the premises, there'd be hell to pay and the pub would be shut down, or possibly burnt down, deemed racist.

When I first visited Wembley, I was overwhelmed by the multiculturalism of the place, it was wonderful. I can never get my head round racism; what bleedin' difference does the colour of our skin or our religious beliefs make? All that matters, surely, is what we are like inside and how kind we are to others. That's why I instantly fell in love with the Wembley culture and Lennys multicoloured group of friends. None of them took a blind bit of notice of skin colour and they all just got on with life. It wasn't like that in Basildon, at that time but it's much better now, I'm happy to say. When Lenny first went to my town centre, he stopped dead in his tracks, mouth open in genuine shock and said, 'Everybody is white.' He had never, in his twenty years of life, seen that before. We only lived fifty miles apart, but the cultural differences were outstanding. When I first walked up the Ealing Road in Wembley, like Lenny, I went into shock but in a different way. Everybody was Asian, we were the only white faces around. I loved it and promised myself that I would visit India one day, which I did many years later, it's still my most favourite country in the whole world. Being turned away from the wine bar that evening shattered my idealistic image of the area. I was being thick really, there is always bound to be an element of racism everywhere; sad but true. The owners only wanted people of certain religions in their bar that night, fair enough, I get that, but I just wish that any business owner, even British ones, could decide who entered their venues. It just doesn't seem fair to me. My Mum used to say, 'Britain is the best country in the world to live in, unless you are British!'. Wise words indeed from my old Mum. Both of my parents were interested in politics. They often used to get very angry whilst watching the news and would actually start shouting at the TV, like that was gonna change anything, bless them. They had seen many changes in their lifetimes and witnessing the downward spiral of their home country, it used to proper upset them.

A couple of years into our relationship, Lenny and I discussed the possibility of renting my house out in Basildon and living with his parents; just to make a bit of extra money more than anything. I am pleased that we didn't follow this plan through because it never would have worked. His Mum and me would have ended up killing each other. Her name was Dot or 'Potty Dotty' as I always called her, but never out loud of course. What a fucking handful she was! Her and Lenny's Dad, Dave, lived in a nice mid-terrace house, decorated in a very nice and classy way. Everything in there was always worth top dollar and she kept it immaculate. Dave was a stereotypical London cabby, he was a big fella, bald head and loved a good old chat. He was a really nice, kind man but was spoken to like shit by his wife, poor sod.

Lenny had a brother, Tony, ten years his senior, who was living with his long-term partner, Penny, in a posh flat in nearby Harrow. Tony and Penny had a few bob because he was a successful builder, had the gift of the gab and a bad case of LBS. He was so different to Lenny in every way. He was a proper Jack the Lad and reminded me of Del Trotter from the TV show 'Only

Fools and Horses'. I found his sick and down to earth humour very amusing but obviously, his LBS irritated me at times. He was a handy bloke to have around if there was any DIY to be done, unlike his little brother. Lenny couldn't even change a light bulb and once spent several hours installing his new car stereo, which didn't turn out quite as he'd hoped. When he had finally fitted it, he took me out in the car to test out his greatest DIY achievement to date. The radio came on as soon as he started the ignition, so all good, until he turned his indicators on and the radio started going on and off in perfect time with the flashing indicator bulb, hysterical but good on him for trying. Lenny seemed to be good at literally everything that he tried, except DIY. I used to tease him about it by calling him 'Reg Prescott' who was a fictional character created by the late, great comedian, Kenny Everett. Reg was the worst DIY man on earth and managed to cut various body parts off during every sketch, very amusing and very Lenny.

Much to my disgust, Lenny was his Mummy's little soldier and she spoilt him something terrible. I know she liked me, she found me amusing, but she tried her very best to fight any nice feelings she had towards me because she knew I was going to take her little boy away from her and hated me for that. I don't know what her problem was, just because I was six years older than him, lived over fifty miles away, had been divorced and was a loud, overconfident Essex girl.........no hang on, perhaps she had a point! He could do no wrong in her eyes and she waited on him hand and foot, to the extent that she used to warm his ugly old fashioned Y-fronts, that she insisted he wore, on the radiator so his bum wouldn't get cold when he put them on in the morning. Oh fuck off, have a word with yaself Potty Dotty!

When he first stayed at my house, I told him that because I had cooked the dinner, he had to wash up. He was twenty years old and it was the first time he had ever done a domestic chore and I knew it because he put half a bottle of washing-up liquid into the water. The first cup that he fished out of the bowl, that was hiding under two foot of bubbles, he placed on the draining board, upright. He didn't even know that cups go upside down when draining. He'd never touched an iron, hoover or washing machine but I made sure that changed pretty sharpish. I may have been older than him but had no intention of replacing his mother as his chief cook and bottle washer. I was too busy for a start and had watched my Mum do way too much for my Dad for the first sixteen years of my life, bollocks to that old malarkey!

Lenny was nothing like Andy, my first husband, who wouldn't let me lift a finger; for some reason he loved being my bitch, very odd. Dot would often remind me how lucky I was that her Lenny loved me and was forever trying to teach me how to cook; good luck with that one. I've got to admit that I take after my Mum where cooking is concerned, she was truly shit at it. If you dared compliment my Mum on the dinner she'd done you, you'd get the same meal for the next five days because she was so chuffed that she'd actually managed to dish up a good one. That was very unusual for a woman of her generation, they are normally excellent in the kitchen, especially at roasts. When the 'Aunt Bessie' range of frozen roast potatoes and Yorkshire puddings came out she was thrilled and so were we! We never had to eat her burnt-on-the- outside and empty-in-the-middle spuds again nor her homemade Yorkshire puddings that my Dad would say he could use as a doorstop or weapon. She hated cooking because she said she had better things to do with her time than be locked in a kitchen, fair play.

Every meal that Dot turned out was fantastic. Our first Christmas together was spent with his lot and I was proper impressed with the food. We even had menus on the perfectly laid out dining room table, that wouldn't have looked out of place at The Ritz. All the grub came from either Harrods or Selfridges; it was amazing. Although the meal was an award winner, the atmosphere seemed strained and there was very little conversation or laughter. This was when I first realised that Dot was battling with alcoholism. Lenny later told me that he had caught his Mum, that very morning, tipping a bit of brandy into her cornflakes and milk. He went mad at her and made her cry, not good. She had been caught, just the week before, with a half-bottle of brandy in her bag whilst at work. She was a receptionist in the local Ford showroom, not acceptable to be greeting new customers while she was stinking of booze and her boss had told her that during the disciplinary meeting the following day. She had been an alcoholic for a few years but not admitted it to anyone, not even herself. Very sad.

My family do Christmas very differently. All the adults are pissed by the time Queenie's speech is aired, which is the only time the TV is on by the way, the rest of the time it's a Chas n Dave, Elvis and Lonnie Donegan knees-up, with lots of singing and dancing. The dinner part of the day is always a bit of an inconvenience with my lot really. We all sit round the table, get the dinner down us, someone will give a speech and mention any loved ones that have died during the year and thank Aunt Bessie for the dinner, clear away and then play games and party.

Lenny's family finished the two-hour long meal, the women cleared and washed up while the men retired to the lounge area to have a brandy and cigar; very refined don't you know but fucking boring! The TV went on and everyone sat in silence, dozing and wondering when Dot was going to go on the turn, due to her having consumed too much alcohol. Fuck me, she went on the turn that year, started shouting at everyone and she chucked the magnificent Christmas tree out of the patio doors and then grabbed hold of me and tried to remove me in the same way she had just removed the bloody tree! It was the first time I had seen her like that, but it wasn't the last. She lost it with me many times but I never once bit, I used to feel sad for her. When she was sober, she was a lovely woman, very respectable but always seemed very unhappy with her life. When she was pissed, she was a fucking nasty piece of work and some! Lenny came to us the following year and said that he had never enjoyed Christmas so much before. He bought his karaoke machine along and attempted to sing his usual slow and romantic songs but got booed off and Chas n Dave went on.

There was no common ground to be found with the two families, which became crystal clear when Dot and Dave invited my parents, sister and brother-in-law, Malcolm, and their four kids to Lenny's twenty-first birthday party, that was to be held in their house. It didn't begin well because Malcolm's car broke down on the M25 on the way to Wembley. Luckily, my Dad managed to fix it, so they did arrive but not on schedule, which stressed Dot out lots. She had put on a magnificent spread, as usual. My motley crew showed up in their Sunday best, except our Malcolm who looked like he was off to the beach in his tricky cap-sleeved t-shirt and lairy shorts. They then proceeded to give my future in-laws the full belt of the Basildon experience. I had never been so proud of my family, they showed Lenny's mob how to have a good time, love them. One of my favourite moments of that day was thanks to Malcolm. When he approached the buffet table, he said to Dot 'What is that weird looking black stuff in the little bowl?'. She informed him, in her best posh voice, that it was caviar. He then put a big old dollop of it, very ungracefully I might add, onto his plate. He tried a bit, pulled a disapproving face and said, 'I've had better!'. What a classic, he obviously meant that he'd had better grub in his gob, but she took it as though he'd had better caviar and the shit she'd purchased from Selfridges, for a small fortune, weren't all that good. He put the icing on the cake when he criticised her 'open sandwiches' by saying to my sister, Chrissie, in a loud voice, 'Dot's rolls ain't got no lids on'. Priceless, way to go Malcolm! Surprisingly, the day turned out to be great. Inevitably, Lenny got the karaoke machine out and started doing a concert. Mainly Lionel Richie hits or as my family call him 'Lionel Rich Tea'; this is because, years ago, Scarlet bought me a mug which had a picture of Lionel on, but his big hair had been replaced by a Rich Tea biscuit and the slogan read, 'Hello, is it tea you're looking for?'. I love that mug, it's my sense of humour down to a tee….see what I did there?

Lenny thought it would melt his audiences' hearts if he serenaded my youngest niece, then only eight months old and all comfy in her little car seat on the floor in the middle of the lounge. Lenny was giving it his all to baby Gracie, entertaining her with his version of 'Hello' whilst everyone else was ignoring him, with the exception of his adoring mother of course. Gracie was liking Lenny's singing at first but then she started to go red. She seemed to be holding her breath and was making strange straining noises. He carried on singing, pretending not to notice what was happening, until she burst into tears when she felt all the hot stuff shoot into her nappy and halfway up her back. The whole room was then engulfed in a shit cloud! She still looked gorgeous, even though she did bleedin' stink. Lenny gave up on the karaoke for a couple of hours after that, but later thought he'd give it another go; this time it was much better, thanks to my Dad.

Apparently, according to my Dad, he had practically invented karaoke or at the very least, it was him that gave them the concept of karaoke! When me and Chrissie were kids, our parents used to go up the Dagenham Working Men's Club and drag us along with them. After he'd downed a few pints, my Dad would blatantly get up on the stage and tell the lead singer of whatever band was playing, that it was his turn to have a little sing now. They never refused him, how could they, he was five foot six! He didn't have the best of voices, but he did have the X factor. His rendition of the Glen Campbell classic 'Rhinestone Cowboy' would always be a good one. My Dad's version being 'Nine-stone Cowboy' and he'd give it everything when singing 'Heart of my Heart' but his closing number would always be 'Knees up Mother Brown'. Oh yeah, he would do a mini concert.

He'd get the whole place up singing and dancing mind, due to his sheer confidence and obvious lust for life; he was a fucking legend my Dad!

His stage presence kicked in big style the day of Lenny's party, that's for sure. When Lenny's 'second act' began, my Dad wasn't having none of it. He grabbed the mike and started 'his' concert. He mixed it up a bit that day and actually started with 'Knees Up Mother Brown' but he changed the lyrics, bless him and sang, 'It's ya twenty-first birthday, let's wake up all the TAN-AH, knees up knees up, don't get the breeze up, knees up Mother BRAN-AH!!!!!'. I couldn't believe my eyes; the cocky little bastard had done it again. All of Lenny's family, his parents, the old Nan and Grandad, aunts, uncles the lot, got off their chairs (I think my Dad may have had to drag a couple of them to their feet) and were singing along and dancing about. They were even doing that linking arms whilst spinning around from one person to the next thing, that you don't see anymore. I used to love that dance; apart from when two people grabbed an arm each and you would be dragged backwards across the dance floor! Lenny stood there watching, his face looked like he'd had a stroke. He had never ever seen his family chuck all their inhibitions out the window and enjoy themselves before. My Dad, with just one song, had managed to drag them down to the gutter to join the rest of us. He later said, 'That was the longest gig that I've ever done!'. It went on for hours and they loved it and we loved it, but Lenny's family never spoke of that night again, what a shame. The only other time our families were together was at mine and Lenny's wedding. They didn't speak to my family at all and seriously looked down their noses at them. Lenny's Mum and aunty even changed the place names on the wedding dinner tables, just so they wouldn't have to eat with my lot. We had all enjoyed a good few hours of fun at Lenny's twenty-first, but instead of embracing that as a good memory, they almost seemed embarrassed about it. How much happier their lives could have been if they'd tried to enjoy themselves more often.

A turning point in mine and Lenny's relationship was when one night, for the first and last time, I dressed up all sexy for him; stockings and all that jazz. I felt that we were growing apart so that was my attempt at getting the spark back into our marriage. We hardly ever spoke anymore because he was always busy, either working, doing his karate thing, playing football, zoned out on his Nintendo or singing to himself on his karaoke machine. He had stopped looking at me, when he sang, a long time ago. I had become a frumpy, nagging, 1950's type housewife, not good. We hadn't had sex for ages and for once, we had the house to ourselves as our lodgers were staying out all night. My plan was, when Lenny got home from work, I would be laying on the sofa, in what I thought was a sexy way. It didn't go well. He walked in, rolled his eyes, frowned, pointed to the bare flesh at the top of my stockings and said, 'What's that?'. I replied 'Cellulite'. That was my fireworks well and truly pissed on, that's for sure! I know for a fact that Nick's reaction to my outfit wouldn't have been cruel, like Lenny's had been. Nick always thought I looked gorgeous and sexy, even with cellulite and he didn't care if I was fat or thin, with or without makeup, he would still fancy me. Lenny's comment and the way he had been treating me for a long while was, here we go again, just like I had said to husband number one years before, 'Unacceptable'!!!!! I had told Lenny many times previously that he was no longer making me feel happy or good about myself. I felt unloved, unattractive and sick of being so low down on his list of priorities and unless he started to acknowledge my existence, I would end our marriage, but he didn't listen. After he'd hit me with that nasty comment, I knew it was the final straw. I went upstairs to change, had a cry, took the very uncomfortable sexy gear off, got dressed and went back down. Lenny was on his Nintendo, quite happy and killing some monster thing on his precious game. I told him that he'd seriously hurt my feelings and that I was going away for a few days to give us both time to think. I had a friend, Linda, who lived in Northampton. I'd met her via Helen, Nick's ex-wife. I had only visited her once before, a long time ago, but I got an overwhelming urge to go and see her. I drove around the corner to the nearest telephone box, phoned her and asked if I could visit. She said that she would be more than happy to put me up for a few days, so off I went. That weekend away turned out to be a life-changer.

Linda was a senior schoolteacher and had the biggest, most amazing tits that I had ever seen. She was a bit conservative, but great fun and was definitely a 'good girl' which was an utter waste of such spectacular boobies, in my opinion. When I arrived at Linda's, she informed me that Helen was also in Northampton that weekend and was staying with her boyfriend, Mick, who lived a short walk from her place. I was chuffed, I hadn't seen Helen for ages and had heard, through the grapevine, that she'd sorted herself out now and was back to her old self again. Mick was on a working visa from Australia; he was short, but no sign of LBS, he was lovely, so laid back and actually looked like an Aussie with his messy blonde hair and rugged complexion. He shared a house with his good friend Ezra, an Israeli Jew who had the sexiest accent I'd ever heard and was tall, dark and handsome to boot.

I fancied Ezra straight away, but then again, who wouldn't? Linda, Helen, Mick, Ezra and I were in one of the many great pubs in Northampton and were having a fab time, when in walked Ezra's girlfriend. She had a face like a smacked arse, and it stayed that way all night. They had not been getting on too good, she told us girls, mainly because Ezra wanted sex all the time and she didn't. I so wanted to say, 'Oh really, you poor thing, it must be terrible having a sex god find you attractive, how awful, you crazy and ungrateful little bitch', but I managed to keep my gob shut. She was a funny girl, who doesn't like a bit of winkle, especially when it's attached to someone who looks like Ezra?! I've got a feeling that she continued with her life, being as miserable as she was that night. I have got a bit of the 'youngest child, princess syndrome' but she had a chronic case

147

of it. She was bringing the mood down and Ezra sensed this, so he took her home.

The rest of us went clubbing and had a seriously good drunken and dancey night. It was nice to spend some time with Helen again. Mick seemed to have calmed her down a bit and she was certainly not off the rails anymore. Mick talked about Helen's children a lot, he seemed besotted with them and with her. We all went back to Mick's house after the club and carried on drinking, dancing, talking shit and drunkenly laughing lots. It must have been three in the morning when Ezra arrived back home, and he told us that he'd dumped old misery bollocks. Good, he would be so much better off with someone else, like me for example. Not to launch into a full-blown relationship with me you understand, but perhaps just to take me upstairs and give me a good seeing-to might be nice. I needed to feel beautiful again. It only took a cheeky wink from me, a sexy twisting motion of my hair with my head on one side, a gentle bite to the corner of my lower lip and finally, a long glance up to the ceiling and we were off upstairs to his bedroom. As we started getting undressed, I noticed he had two bad scars, one on his upper thigh and one on the back of his lower leg. When I asked about them, like you do when you're about to get it on with a gorgeous Jewish hunk and set in stone the end of your second marriage, he casually answered in his broken English 'I get shot two times in leg when in national service in Israel'. What a fucking MAN! He suddenly looked even more desirable, if that was at all possible. We were very good together in that department, he was a lot more loving in bed than I would have expected. I thought we would have just bumped uglies, but there was real emotion there and I wasn't sure if I liked that really. I was in desperate need to feel sexy again but nothing else.

The next day, I said my goodbyes to the Northampton lot and headed back home to tell Lenny what I had done. I felt sick at the very thought of confessing, but the marriage had been over long before the Ezra episode and I think we both knew it. I could not cope with his immaturity, neglect or selfish ways any longer, without going potty. I had gone to Northampton with newspaper in my boots to stop the rain from getting in through the holes in the soles. Days before, Lenny had come home with a new Nintendo game that had cost a fortune. I could have got two pairs of boots for what he'd paid for yet another stupid game. When I asked him if he knew that I was in desperate need of new boots, he just shrugged, pulled a sad face like a child and said that all his mates thought that it was the best game ever though. When I got back from Northampton, he didn't even ask me if I'd had a nice time or if I was okay. He glanced at me, only taking his eyes off his game for a second and just said 'Hiya' as though I had just returned from the local shop. He wasn't moody, angry or sulking, I don't think he'd even noticed that I hadn't been there. The house was spotless when I had left but now it was a shithole. He'd only been on his own since the night before. He'd cooked, made a terrible mess and not even taken his empty bowls or plates into the kitchen, let alone washed them up. What was I supposed to do, clear up his mess, cook him a dinner, confess my sins, swear my undying love for him and spend the rest of my life as his invisible slave, not fucking likely! I stood in front of the TV and he did an exaggerated swerve to one side, to enable him to continue playing his game, and had both of his hands gripping the Nintendo control pad as though his life would end if he dared to let go of it. I told him I was going away again and that I'd had sex with another man, our marriage was over, and I wanted him and his stuff out of my house by the time I got back in three days' time. He asked where I was going and I said, 'Back to Northampton of course.' I got into my car and was shaking like a leaf because I didn't think our chat was going to go quite like that, I was gutted. I did love him very much and just wanted him to love me back, but I knew that was never going to happen. That was that then, another one bites the dust.

Where to now? Ezra's of course. In this day and age, I would have texted him to prewarn him, but that wasn't an option for me in the late 1990's, so I just turned up. Ezra did have a mobile phone, as did several of my friends, but I was never very good, and still ain't, with anything new or technical. I really have got some front sometimes me; I amaze myself. Thankfully, when I arrived in Northampton, Ezra answered the door and it was immediately obvious that he was pleased to see me, in more ways than one! I was in desperate need of a cuddle and he gave me one….see what I did there? The next few days that Ezra and I spent together, were pretty strange. Ezra was a real lady's man, loved playing the field, had broken many a heart and had never been in love. We did have some good laughs and great sex, but when it was time to go home, I didn't feel any need, or desire, to make arrangements for another date. I had a divorce to organise, a house to sell and to sort my shit out in general. Ezra, on the other hand, didn't feel the same way. The silly bastard had only gone and fallen hook, line, and sinker for me. It was bloody inconvenient to be honest. I really didn't need another scene; I was mentally raped already. I told him how sorry I was that I didn't feel the same, but he said that he would make me love him and insisted I went to see him again in a week or two. I agreed because it was the timing of us meeting that was bad, not him. I just wasn't ready for another relationship, but I gave it a go.

Unfortunately, the inner anger I had regarding Lenny not wanting to try to save our marriage and forcing me to be a two-time divorcee at the age of thirty-two, all came out and hit Ezra with full force. Never would I describe myself as a bitch, but I was to him. I treated him even worse than I had treated Andy and I didn't think I had it in me to do that. Perhaps it was Ezra's karma for all the hearts he'd broken over the years, he certainly knows how he had made those girls feel now if that is the case or is that just me trying to justify my atrocious behaviour! Ezra took me and my parents out for dinner one night and a horrible thing happened. Words can't explain how much I loved and respected my wonderful Mum and Dad and how I always did everything in my power to make them proud of me, which they were, but not that night. They thought Ezra was totally charming, kind, funny, great company and they were right. During that meal, I criticised everything that Ezra said, constantly put him down and mugged him off about his, not so good, English. When Ezra went to the loo at the end of the evening, my Mum told me that my manners and the way I spoke to that lovely man were shocking and that her and my Dad were ashamed of me. I deserved to feel bad, I was one nasty bastard the entire evening. When my Mum died, many years later, we found Ezra's business card in her purse; how sweet that she had kept it for all that time. Nick was always my parents' favourite, but she obviously saw something in Ezra that touched her heart. I packed him in soon after that, I hated the side of me that he was bringing out and he deserved better.

I sold the house and had to give Lenny half of the profit, it wasn't much, or I would have kicked up a stink. He'd come to the party with fuck all, therefore it would have been an injustice if he'd had loads of money off me. I got myself a little flat in Basildon but started getting the urge to go travelling, but then Lenny became ill. The divorce was underway, so it shouldn't have been any of my business really, but he made it so. He was later diagnosed with paranoid schizophrenia, but at the time I just thought he'd gone fucking mental! After he'd left me, he moved into digs with some friends from his work, in Southend. We hadn't been in touch since the split, apart from via a solicitor, but we had mutual friends, Cliff and Donna. They were a lovely couple but a strange pair. Cliff was a cross-dresser, before it became fashionable! Ann was fine about her husband's occasional need to wear women's clothes and even used to help him with his make-up when they went for their monthly nights out to a club called 'Trans-Essex.' Lenny and I had gone to their club with them one night, but I hated it. I really enjoyed socialising with the many transgender people that were there, and Cliff looked amazing as a woman, but I kept getting the feeling that everyone assumed that I was a bloke, dressed as a woman and that Lenny was my gay partner. If Lenny had of dressed as a woman, he would have looked stunningly beautiful, with his high cheekbones, long eyelashes and slim build; lucky bastard. It's a pretty safe bet to say that he would have looked much better in a Lycra dress than I would have done at that particular time because I was going through a fat phase again. Cliff and Donna had told me that they'd seen Lenny several times during the few months that we had been separated, and he was doing fine; I was genuinely pleased for him.

I got home from doing an Ann Summers party late one night, only days after my chat with Cliff and Donna, and the phone was ringing in my flat. I thought someone must have died, they hadn't, thankfully. However, it was my poor Mum on the phone, and she sounded upset and said I was to drive to theirs immediately because Lenny was with them and was acting very strange. Something had snapped in Lenny's head and he had decided that all he needed in his world was me, so he had done no more than to start walking from his place in Southend to Basildon, a twelve-mile journey! He did have a car, but he now considered that to be an unnecessary item. It was freezing that night and there were remnants of frozen slush on the ground, left over from the snow a couple of days before. En route, he had removed and discarded into various roadside bushes, his shoes, socks, clothes (except for his thin shirt and trousers), wallet containing money and credit cards, his house and car keys and apparently, his mind too! He was now sat on my parent's sofa, clinging onto a nice hot cup of tea, his sore feet in the washing up bowl that my Mum had filled with warm, bubbly water, a blanket around his shoulders and had our Basil on his lap. Even the dog knew there was something wrong, he was looking at his Daddy in a proper odd way. I didn't really know what to do, I felt terrible that my parents were having to go through this and totally helpless where Lenny was concerned. I sat next to him and gave him a cuddle, while he sat silently sobbing until he went into a deep sleep on the sofa, with me next to him wide awake.

The next day I took him to his flat, luckily one of his house mates was there to let us in. There was a note for Lenny in his bedroom from the police, asking him to call them, which I did for him. Several people had seen him on his half-marathon the night before, were concerned, so called the police, who were brilliant by the way. They had managed to retrace his steps and retrieved almost all his possessions but alas, his mind was still nowhere to be found! We then went to my flat, which turned out to be a mistake. He wouldn't even sit down because he was frightened of the plug sockets. It was via them that the people that wanted his soul watched his every move and listened to everything that he said. Too many episodes of the 'X Files' had been watched by my crazy ex-husband I was thinking. I had to get out of there, so I suggested we go for a drive. My plan was to take him to his parents for help and moral support. He insisted on driving and I was stupid enough to let him, another big mistake. Eight hours later we arrived in Scotland, seriously. I managed to find a hotel for us to stay in and when we got into our hotel room he said that he felt safer because he was far enough away from 'those people' so he could tell me everything; oh fucking great, I could hardly wait!!!! 'Those people' control everything apparently, even the birds. Every species of bird is in fact a crow in disguise and they report our every move to 'them'. Lenny was sure that 'they' would get all of our souls in the end and give them to the devil himself. All righty then! This went on for hours, him speed-talking some seriously weird shit. The next morning, I drove him to his Mum and Dad's, who were so angry with me because they thought that I had made him like this, and they kicked me out of the house. Fucking good, thank you, that was the kindest thing they had ever done for me.

I didn't hang about after all that, I packed my bags and flew to Spain. I got an apartment and a job in Benidorm, all on that same day. That sounds unbelievably impressive, but I had lived in that apartment block and worked in the same bar several years before, when Andy and I split up the first time round. It was just after we had sold the marital home that I went travelling and spent some of the equity but, I was sensible, and left enough to buy my little one bedroom place in Basildon when I returned. I did Spain, Portugal, Greece and Italy. What a great time I had, I was as free as a Basbird back then, had a few quid in my purse and it helped to heal my broken heart after Andy had sodded off. I had started my eight-month stint in Benidorm but soon realised that getting a two-month lease on an apartment and a bar job was okay, but it felt as though life was as routined as being at home. Consequently, I did hostels from then on because you can always get work in them as a cleaner or on reception to get free accommodation, thus making your money last a bit longer. It's also more fun because you are always surrounded by people who are in the same situation as you and everyone shares tips on where to go sightseeing and to party. When you travel alone, which so many backpackers do, you are never lonely because everyone misses their families, so you tend to get very close to your new friends, they almost become your substitute family, it's wonderful.

I felt very relieved to have left Lenny and all the dramas back home and to be back in Benidorm; I was loving life again. I really liked my little apartment, liked working back in the bar and I felt very content being single. That feeling didn't last long because on the fifth day, there was a knock on my door and there was Lenny, still with crazy eyes, clutching nothing other than his passport. What the fucking fuck!! He had phoned my parents, hours before from the airport, unbeknown to my Mum of course, and said that he wanted my address in Spain to enable him to write to me to thank me for helping him and to apologise for his recent behaviour. They believed him and gave him my new address, so now here he was in my new apartment. He said that when I had kicked him out of the house, many months before, I had turned him into a gay man, and he hated being that way. He said he would kill me and then himself, unless I gave us another go. He emphasized this point by dangling off my balcony, which was eight floors up. I was proper frightened. I said everything he wanted to hear, he calmed down and went to sleep.

I didn't want to be alone with him so, the next morning, I got him some swimmers and made him come to the crowded Benidorm beach with me; safety in numbers and all that. Yet again, that was a mistake. He just stood there staring at all the sunbathing folk and then totally lost it big time. He started actually screaming and pointing to a little sparrow, who was minding his own business hopping about on the hot sand. 'That's them' he shouted, 'They are even watching me here.' He was pacing up and down on the beach, squeezing his head and muttering to himself. It was so sad to see him like that; it broke my heart. It's a good job we were in Benidorm because nobody seemed to take a blind bit of notice. They just assumed he was yet another low-life Brit who had got on it too early. I took him back to my apartment, packed, got in a cab and headed straight to the airport. That was the shortest travelling experience I have had to date. It wasn't the horrendous journey back to the UK that finally pushed 'me' over the edge, it was when we got back to my flat in Basildon and he started smashing all my things up. I didn't care about that, it's only stuff, but I did care, very much indeed, that Basil was so frightened, and his pads were cut to shreds from the broken glass that was all over the carpet. He was bleeding and yelping with pain. Again, I said all the right things, Lenny calmed down, we sorted the dog out and then he agreed that he needed help. I wasn't the right person to help him, his parents and the doctors done that. He got diagnosed and put on the right medication for his illness. The divorce got finalised and I never saw him again.

Chapter 6 We had a moment, I met Gavin and his friends

I was gutted that my Spanish fun had been cut short and that I had spunked all my savings, due to Lenny's mental health problems. There I was, back in Basildon in my little smashed up flat, skint, unemployed and on the bones of my arse. I was totally lost and didn't know what to do next. I know, I'll go to Helen and Mick's wedding, see Nick there, finally tell him how much I love him and about the plan I had for our future together all those years ago, listen to how he feels the same and that he thinks we should never of let each other go and end the heartbreaking chat with the fact that there is nothing that we can do about it now because he is with Dawn and they have got two kids. Yep, that just about done it, I hit rock bottom. Life can be such a proper shit at times can't it?!

Helen and Mick weren't just getting married, but they were also emigrating to Australia and taking Nick's four eldest children with them. I had a word with myself that night because as crap as I felt, poor Nick's situation was a thousand times worse. He idolises his kids, they are his world and he was just about to lose four of them, awful. He didn't put up a fight because he had been brain washed, like many people, into thinking the old classic 'They will have a much better life over there.' What a load of bollocks that is. What part of the planet we live on doesn't govern how happy our lives are going to be; that's just geography isn't it? Does it really make a difference to our mental well-being if the weather is hot or cold? If we live near the sea or on a council estate? In a mansion or a mud hut? That matters not a jot, does it? Surely, it's the people that are in our own little worlds and the amount of love and kindness that we give and receive, is what is going to make us happy or sad? It really pisses me off when people tell me that they are leaving their parents, siblings, aunts, uncles, friends and everyone else that loves and cares about them because they think that they, and their children in some cases, will be much happier thousands of miles away from the massive ball of love they are currently living in because apparently, 'It's a much better way of life where we're going'. Oh fuck off and listen to yourselves, open your eyes and appreciate what is around you now. So what if you will be able to live in a big posh house if you leave, do yourselves a favour, don't go, stay with the wonderful people that you have been blessed with and live somewhere, perhaps smaller and stop being so materialistic, flash and fucking greedy. However, I understand when someone emigrates because they have fallen in love with somebody from another country and they want to be together, they have no choice then, they have to pick one of their countries to live in. That must be so hard, and I feel for them. I also get it if someone isn't surrounded by a loving family and friends and they want to move away. Go for it, knock yourself out because your happiness may well be waiting for you elsewhere and there's only one way to find out and that is by fucking off! Oh my days, that was a rant and a half wasn't it?! I feel worn out now. I must point out that although I have done a lot of travelling in my life, I always return to my loved ones in the end. I do practice what I preach.

I'm sorry to say that Dawn was never overly-interested in Helen and Nick's children; she wasn't too keen on the step-mum role and although she did go through the motions with them, doing what she had to do, she always saw them as a bit of an inconvenience. The news that they were being taken to the other side of the world, suited her just fine. It was near the end of Helen and Mick's wedding reception, during a slow dance, that Nick and I had our second conversation of the night because

167

obviously talking about our missed opportunity in the first chat hadn't been heart-wrenching enough. He told me that him and Dawn were not happy, she had already cheated on him and they were constantly at each other's throats and she had given him no emotional support regarding the forthcoming loss of his eldest children. Everything was shit and we agreed that we just weren't destined to be together, sad but true.

All the heartache that Nick had endured in the build-up to the kids emigrating, turned out to be in vain. Mick went back to Australia on his own at first, to sort the accommodation out for his newfound family and Helen and the kids followed, three weeks later. Nick went to the airport to wave them off. He was in floods of tears because he never knew when he would see his four eldest kids again. In the three weeks that Helen and Mick were apart, she shagged one of Mick's, so called, good friends, Andrew. She decided that the Andrew shag was a mistake and went to Australia, with the kids in tow and didn't tell her new husband what had happened. The big house that Mick had got for them all was apparently very nice, but they never hung about long enough to enjoy it because just a few days after they had moved in, guess who showed up on the doorstep, oh yes, Andrew. He told Mick everything and announced his love for Helen; the two of them then fucked off and left Mick with the kids! I know Mick was laidback, but he was being proper mugged off and some right? Helen, Andrew and the kids flew back to the UK a few days later and moved straight back into her council house with her new boyfriend, like nothing had happened. She hadn't informed the council that they were emigrating because she had rent arrears and was just going to let them find out in their old sweet time that she had buggered off. Nick was delighted but Dawn wasn't too chuffed, and life carried on.

I didn't see Nick again for years, but I did meet the legend that was 'Gavin' and we spent the next five years living or travelling abroad. Gavin was the funniest bugger that I've ever met, or ever likely to; his sense of humour was second to none. Our paths first crossed when he walked into the mobile phone shop that I was working in as an accounts administrator. I had turned in my career in retail, I had to really because I had become too outspoken and this was now unacceptable with all the new 'political correctness' shit that had come about. Working with the public was no longer an option for the gobby, foul-mouthed, opinionated old bint that I had become.

That mobile phone shop was the funniest place I have ever worked, mainly because my dear friend Lauren had got me the job and she is the second funniest person that I have ever met! Working with her was literally a laugh a minute. Lauren, like many of my friends, is beautiful and sexy with an outgoing and flirty personality. My girlfriends all used to love a lowcut top with tits almost out, short skirts, lots of make-up and looked a bit tarty, but gorgeous with it. Lauren used to say that her contribution to motherhood was wearing knickers on a night out, funny fucker! It's strange really because in my experience of working for Ann Summers for years and having been on many a girlie night out, that girls that dress and act in that way are normally 'good girls'. They just like dressing up like that because looking sexy makes them feel good about themselves and boosts their self-esteem. It doesn't mean that they want a good seeing-to at the end of the night! When we all used to go on a girlie one, I know for a fact that blokes would look at me and my friends and say, 'They will all be up for a shag, except for the one in the Hush Puppies'. They were completely wrong because my friends would only sleep with men that they had got to know well and liked; they took sex very seriously. They used to say that it was a pointless and unenjoyable act unless they had feelings for the bloke and they would rather have an extra spud on their roast dinner, rather than sleep with a stranger. Me however, the Hush Puppy wearer, thought differently. I couldn't understand why they all took it so seriously. Sex was just a bit of free entertainment, good exercise and could be very enjoyable, even if it wasn't with, what you thought, might be your future husband. I still can't see why most people have so many hang ups about it to be honest. I can totally understand the transgender thing but, the only difference with me is that I like having a noony, but I do tend to 'think' like a man where sex is concerned. I do not associate sex with love you see, I think love comes from your heart, not your genitals. I have been told that I am a gay man, who is trapped inside a woman's body; I am happy with that because I don't have to have any surgery or change my name or title with my kind of transgenderism.

Gavin was visiting our mobile phone shop to see if he could sell us some advertising space in the local newspaper, who he was working for then. When Gavin first saw me and Lauren, we were giggling like naughty schoolgirls and rolling along the corridor floor bursting a roll of giant bubble wrap with whatever body part hit first. It was all in a day's work and there's worse ways of spending your lunch break. There was absolutely no sexual chemistry between Gavin and I, but the soul bond and the love of a good bit of banter was immediately apparent. He was a funny looking sod, a bit pigeon chested, only about two inches off of having LBS, legs a bit too short for his body and there was a bit of the 'Jimmy Hills' going on in the chin area but with a personality like his, who would care, including him? He was born and brought up in super-rich folk territory, Hutton in Essex or 'Hut-Ta-Tun' as he used to say it. He'd been public school educated and had a posh accent, that he could turn on or off, depending on the company he was keeping. His parents had divorced a few years before. His Mum had been a housewife and his Dad was an accountant that had run off with his secretary; I've never heard of that happening before! The big posh family house had been sold and his Mum bought a small two bedroom house in Hornchurch and Gavin was still living there with her. He was the baby of the family and had two older brothers. The three of them had all attended 'Brentwood Boys Public School'. The eldest, James, had left school, gone to university and was

173

now a qualified accountant, like his father, and living happily in London with his long-term partner and their young daughter. The second eldest, Simon, had also followed in the family's accountancy tradition, had completed his degree at the same university as his older brother, but had decided to do a bit of travelling before launching into working life. He had gone for a standard medical before he was heading off to Australia and was diagnosed with lymphatic cancer. He lived for another torturous two years, but sadly lost his long and painful battle with cancer. He was only in his mid-twenties when he died.

It was during Simon's illness that the Dad buggered off with the secretary. Gavin's poor Mum was a neurotic woman, even before the double loss that she had been forced to endure, but that had made her actually go nuts. She was such a lovely woman and very, very posh. When her husband left, she had vowed never to entertain another man again and now spent almost all her time protesting to keep our English independence. She was a well-educated lady and where politics were concerned, knew her stuff. Nothing made her happier than talking about political issues and going on her many peaceful protests. If she had of been born sooner, she would have been one of the amazing suffragettes, that's for sure. Her dress sense was terrible; she always wore bright coloured clothes that looked expensive, but she had no bleedin' idea which colours went with which. She was the Queen of Clash and used to dye her slightly scruffy hair, bright orange; she was a true eccentric. I thought she was excellent, but she annoyed the hell out of Gavin. The only time that I ever saw him pissed off was when he was with his Mum. He disagreed with her

politics and almost every other opinion she had. We often had an argument when we had visited his Mum because I thought the way that he used to talk to her sometimes was outrageously bad. Yes, she was crazy but for fuck's sake, who wouldn't be after losing a son to cancer and a husband to a secretary, give the poor

175

woman a break. James and Gavin both used to get frustrated with their Mum. I think it hurt their hearts, seeing their Mum so fucked up by her shitty life. This made them feel helpless and angry, so, for some reason, they took it out on her, not good. I could understand their actions to a point because she was hard work and used to eat with her mouth open, making the most god-awful slapping, chomping noises. My Dad made the same noises when he ate. It used to make my nerves bad listening to those two eat. Thank fuck I never dined with them both at the same time, I would not have been able to hear myself think; feeding time at the zoo! She did have terrible mood swings too and cried hysterically if anyone mentioned Simon's name which was heart wrenchingly sad to witness. Gavin used to literally put his head in his hands sometimes because she tended to change the subject a couple of times during each sentence which almost drove him to distraction. Having said all that, I must add that she was a good soul, kind, thoughtful and adored her sons and granddaughter. She thought I was great too; if I swore or used slang, she used to clap her hands very fast in front of her face and say in her posh voice, 'Oh Jackie, you are so wonderfully common.' Apart from Gavin's attitude towards his Mum, I thought everything about him was the bollocks.

The day Gavin and I met, he said that he would like to take me out for the day that Saturday. He made it perfectly clear that it wasn't a date because I was too thin, my boobs were not big enough, I was way too common for him, but he thought we would have a laugh; fair enough. I agreed and he took me to Frinton, which is officially the most boring town in the UK and the only one that didn't have a pub (it has now by the way). He soon realised that he had done a wrong-un and suggested we walked along the coast to Walton-on-the-Naze, where I had gone with my second boyfriend, Charlie, for my first ever dirty weekend, almost twenty years before. Walton was also one of my favourite places to go on holiday when I was a kid. My parents had a few bob, because my Dad was a pipefitter and used to travel all over the world to earn a good living. He'd worked in Israel, Venezuela, America, Iran, Saudi Arabia and shitloads of other places. Of course, my Dad had a successful career because he had LBS! Every year, from when I was a baby, we would holiday once abroad and then again in the UK. It's amazing that the holidays that me and Chrissie have the fondest memories of, are the ones that we spent in the UK. Our favourites being at the Warners Holiday Camp on the Isle of Wight and at the Martello Caravan Park at good old Walton-on-the-Naze. Chrissie actually met her first husband there, Burt, when they were both just seventeen. They had a teenage holiday romance but ended up getting married. It's thanks to Walton that my nieces, Scarlet and Rosie, were born!

Me and Gavin had a nice walk along the seafront, and he didn't moan one bit when I made him visit the Martello Caravan Park as I wanted to have a little reminisce. I was gutted because the camp had turned into a right shithole, full of low-life and was looking a bit shabby but it still brought some happy memories flooding back. On the walk back to Frinton, Gavin bought six wonderfully fattening, hot ring-doughnuts and passed the bag to me. I was chatting away, picking at the doughnuts, then he asked me to pass him one. When I reached into the bag, to my horror, I realised that I had scoffed the lot. This was the birth of Gavin's pet name for me; 'TigPig'. When I asked him to explain why he had just called me that, he said that I reminded him of Tigger from Winnie-the-Pooh because I was bouncy, bouncy, fun, fun, fun, fun, fun, and that I was a greedy fat pig for demolishing all the doughnuts. I became his very own 'Tig-Pig' from that day on and he never called me anything else again. When he dropped me off at my flat, neither of us felt the urge to have a kiss but we agreed that we wanted to spend loads more time together. This friendship went on for months. We became inseparable and we just never stopped talking and laughing. His quick wit and the way we bounced off each other, was constantly entertaining. It was possibly the most I had ever laughed and had never felt happier. My heart used to almost pound out of my chest when we were due to meet, from pure excitement and anticipation of what the next few hours would bring.

Gavin and I had been good friends for three months, when something wonderful happened. We'd been out for dinner and he had popped into mine for a coffee. He seemed a bit anxious, so I asked him if everything was okay. 'Not really' he said and got up to leave. I felt sick, I thought I had said something to piss him off. He then told me that for the first time ever, he had fallen in love. NOOOO!!! When'd he had the time to meet someone else? I hated her already, or is it a man, oh no, he's gay, she or he was gonna take my Gavin away from me, the bitch! the bastard! I tend to show all my feelings in my face, so he knew what was going through my mind so, quickly, he told me that he was in love with ME. I am such a fucking idiot at times, and this was definitely one of those times because I said, 'But we don't fancy each other?', nice one Jackie! He said that he had never felt like this about anyone before, so he wanted to give us a go romantically and he had a plan. He thought that we should have a snog and that he was gonna put his tongue in my gob and everything. If it repulsed us, then we would never speak of it again; sounded like a good plan to me. I was hoping it wouldn't be one of those kisses where it felt as though the bloke was trying to lick the bottom of a yoghurt pot, because I hated that. So, he brought on the snog. That first kiss was magical, he melted me, inside and out and he felt the same way. We didn't launch into full blown sex, like I wanted to. He simply said 'Wow, we'll continue this another time my gorgeous little Tig-Pig' and left.

The next time Gavin and I got together it felt a bit awkward. For a start, we'd had an Indian meal and I was dying to blow off. I had always blown off in front of him before the kiss and used to laugh my head off afterwards. I love a bit of toilet humour and a good loud blow off, but now I felt as though I should act more ladylike. My Mum hated my public blow offs and she used to tell me that men would never truly respect me if I broke wind in their presence. I know she had a point, but I was born ill and have had more medical issues than anyone else I've ever known. One of my problems is a blockage in my oesophagus so I am unable to burp, and the wind has got to come out somewhere, so I blow off. It is what it is.

My parents had been married for thirty-two years at the time and my Mum had never blown off in front of my Dad, or anyone come to that, but then one night, she had a mishap. Back in the day you used to have to get off your arse to change the television channel. How she must have wished that remote controls had of been invented on that fateful evening. Me and Andy had gone to visit my parents and the four of us were sitting in the lounge, watching a bit of telly. My Mum got up to turn the TV over when, I ain't joking, she cracked-off a showstopping fart. It lasted the entire journey from the sofa to the TV, a good four seconds.

After she'd farted her way across the room, she changed the channel, hesitated for a bit, obviously wanting the floor to swallow her up at that point, turned and quickly walked back to the sofa, her face all red. We all sat in silence for a while because, as much as we wanted to burst out laughing, we knew that she must have been dying inside with embarrassment. Silence now and to never mention it, like ever, was the best way to go, but my Dad, the old git, disagreed. He said, 'Bloody hell Rose, that was thirty-two years' worth wasn't it?' and started laughing. Mass hysteria then occurred in the room, but my Mum didn't laugh, she just said 'Pardon me.' She never done another one in front of my Dad and their marriage lasted another twenty-seven years; until death did they part.

Whenever I had started a new sexual relationship, I would never spend the night with the bloke because of something my Dad once said: 'My Jackie must have very tight skin because if she falls asleep on my sofa, her eyes shut and her arse opens.' Now I consider that a 'classic Dad line' but it must have planted a seed in my head because I always refused to sleep-over with a new lover because I didn't relish the thought of dropping my guts when I went to sleep in the arms of a man who I'd just had sexy-time with. Call me old fashioned if you will, but that's just the way I am!! One night I had gone back to some blokes house and he insisted that I stayed over, but I ended up not getting any shut-eye at all because every time I needed to blow off I went to the toilet, pulled my bum cheeks apart and muffled the sound with tissue; seriously, it just wasn't worth the aggro. When I've been seeing them for a while, and we get on 'farting terms' that's a game changer and I don't care if one slips out. I'd even start saying things after I had done one like, 'There's one I didn't want' or 'Get out and walk' or the old beauty 'More tea Vicar?'. Everyone a winner! I know it's childish, but it really makes me laugh, I can't help it. Even if I do a loud one and I'm on my own, I still laugh. Not many things in life are enjoyable and free but blowing off and shagging are two of those rare and precious things; never to be done at the same time though. It seemed to work in reverse with Gavin and I, we were on farting terms and now we weren't. I could say anything to Gavin, so after the Indian meal and when my trapped wind started to actually hurt me, I said, 'Unless I rip one off right now, I am going to explode.' So, I did it, on his request mind; it was a corker and we both laughed. He then let one go, not as good as mine but he had the ability to burp, in fact he could burp the alphabet up to the letter 'M' which he was very proud of but his fart was good enough to enable us to laugh even harder. That turned out to be the most mental 'foreplay' that I had ever encountered; filth really but hey-ho. We made love for the first time that night. Please note that I said, 'made love' and not my usual crude terminology.

We were perfect together, now in every way, I loved him so much. I still hadn't met Gavin's Dad and his partner (the secretary) or any of his friends. He explained that he loved his friends, but they were all ex-public school boys and total snobs who used to crack regular jokes about Basildon people. Mugging us all off as though the entire town was full of nothing but low-life. They had even warned Gavin not to go out with 'one of those Basildon people'. He took me to meet them in a club in Brentwood, home of 'The Only Way is Essex' on the telly. I instantly hated the venue, it was full of rich pretentious twats in expensive outfits, talking posh and way too loudly, swinging their arms about dramatically as if to say 'Look at me, aren't I gorgeous?' whilst tossing their perfectly styled hair. I was still a hippy and felt very out of place.

When he introduced me to his friends, they were all holding various cocktails and stood around an expensive tall glass table, next to the dance floor. Fair play to them, they didn't try to hide the fact that they thought that I was a commoner, nor that they were hoping that Gavin would grow out of his phase of wanting to sleep with a Basildon girl. They didn't hold back, one by one they 'interviewed' me. The fact that I had already managed to get divorced twice went down like a cup of cold sick and one of them even said, trying to be nice I think, 'I have heard that there are still a few nice parts of Basildon.' When I told them that I drove a Ford Fiesta they blatantly laughed. Even on the dance floor I clocked them looking at my moves and then looking at each other and openly laughing. I love a boogie me and really do dance as though nobody is watching, but they were making me feel very self-conscious. I was feeling that they were better than me and perhaps I should try to be more like them to impress Gavin. I even considered mimicking their dance moves, but they danced like everybody 'was' watching and that ain't me.

I had to pee so left the uncomfortable dance floor and headed to the loo. To my horror there were two posh birds snorting cocaine off the shelf by the toilet sinks. I had never seen anyone do that in public before. I thought it was terrible behaviour, so I gave them my best disapproving 'Penelope Pinchface' look and went for a wee. When I returned to the group, they were standing around the table again. Gavin's old school friend, Rupert, sorry to go on about it but an LBS sufferer, reached across the table and squeezed Kay's left boob and asked, 'Your boobies look big tonight Kay, have you had them done?'. Rupert was also Leonard's old school chum and the following week Rupert was going to be the best man at Leonard and Kay's wedding. Rupert had just cupped the tit of the bride-to-be. What the hell! Leonard was gonna beat the living crap out of him, but no, he just laughed, as did Kay. For fuck's sack, these people are public school educated, surely for the amount of dosh their parents had forked out for them to go there, they would have been taught manners and common decency, for crying out loud! Rupert was Leonards best man and he has just groped his future wife, right in front of him and in public! To make it worse, he then leant forward again but this time his tiny little LBS hand was heading towards my left tit. All I did was gently knock his hand away and say 'Rupert, if ever you want to touch any part of my body, especially a boob, please ask my permission first.' One would assume that he would understand that simple request but no, what did the little posh prick do? He did an overexaggerated step backwards, slowly opened his small arms, really wide and said, 'Oh no, I have offended the Basildon girl, what is she going to do, hit me?'. Too fucking right she is, you arrogant wanker. My Grandad was a keen bareknuckle boxer in the 1920's and I tell ya, he would have been well proud of me. I caught him right under his detestable little chin and his tiny putrid body lifted right up into the air and then fell to the floor. 'That'll fucking teach ya, you horrible stuck-up tosser!' I thought. I was shaking and couldn't even look at Gavin. I grabbed my bag, glanced at Rupert, who was still laying on the floor with his small face looking all shocked and I walked out. I didn't know the Brentwood area and started desperately looking for a taxi rank, thinking that there probably wasn't one because they'd all be picked up by their chauffeurs later. Then I felt a gentle tap on my shoulder and there was Gavin. He said, 'I have never been as proud of anyone as I

189

am of you right now, I love you my Basbird.' Later he told me that if I hadn't of laid Nick out, he would have done, so I had saved him a job!

The following week I went to Leonard and Kay's wedding, as Gavin's plus one, and Rupert apologised to me but apparently, he never did apologise to Kay for the titting-up that she had received on that eventful night, when 'Basildon' met 'Brentwood'! From that day to this, I have never judged people by their financial status, education or accents again. I now know that there are good and bad people in every walk of life. Shame on me, for that short time, thinking that their richness and poshness made them better than me; I have never made that mistake again.

Gavin moved into my flat and we couldn't have been happier. We did everything together, but we decided that because we were both so excellent, that we should go international. He had been backpacking many times before, but this had disappointed his Father because he thought that Gavin should further his education and 'make something of himself'. Gavin had lived in Australia for a year and loved it, his dream was to live there permanently but he had no family there and no career, so it was just a dream. I was gutted for him but pleased for myself because I didn't want to live anywhere other than the UK or anywhere that was away from him. When he'd been there previously, he had got a working visa, but you can only have one of those in your lifetime. I, however, did have family living there, my Aunt Becky, one of my Dad's seven sisters. She had emigrated in the 1960's on one of the famous ten pound crossings with her new husband. They stayed there and were later blessed with their two children.

My Dad's parents were very upset when Becky left the UK, but my Dad was quite happy at the time, because it meant that there was one less woman at home. When Becky told her parents that she was moving away, her Dad didn't speak to her ever again.

They continued to live in the same house for several weeks after her announcement, and she often tearfully begged him to talk to her, but he would just silently look away. On the day she left, she said her final goodbyes to her family, but her Dad stormed out of the house without saying a word. She told me that when she was on the ship, minutes before it sailed away, it was like something out of a sad film. The passengers were all lined up on the top deck, waving to their loved ones on the dock below, who were shouting, waving flags and holding up 'Good Luck' banners. She was desperately trying to spot her new husband's family in the crowds of people on the dockside, when she spotted him - her Dad! He was stood there waving and it was obvious that he couldn't see his daughter in the line of hundreds of people on the ship, but he continued to wave frantically and kept blowing kisses. How heartbreaking that he had got his head around her move just a little bit too late. He missed his chance to have one last cuddle with her. Unfortunately, they never saw each other again, but they did keep in touch by letter, until he died a few years later.

It must have been difficult for my Dad and Grandad, having to live with eight females! Apparently, the two of them often used to have to leave the house in a pair of knickers because they could never find a pair of pants in the mountain of disorganised clothes. My Dad's childhood home was not only total chaos, but a bit dirty too. My Grandad had to do all the domestic chores because my Nan, although a mother of eight, didn't have a clue; she was like a child herself. If my Grandad gave her money to do the shopping she would come back with no dinners, just cakes, biscuits and sweets. He had to do all the housework because she wasn't good at that either, which is surprising because as a kid she had been in and out of the orphanage and at the age of thirteen she had gone into service, as a scullery maid. That's how she had met my Grandad. He used to deliver the bread to the big posh old house that she worked and lived in, downstairs in the basement of course. He was obviously delivering more than the bread because my Nan got pregnant and her employers, a Lord and Lady, paid for her to get married, so as not to shame the household. My Grandad even knitted the baby clothes and of course worked long hours, as a postman, to bring the money in too. It's no wonder he didn't make old bones, but she lived until she was well into her nineties. He had emphysema but it was just called 'bad bronchitis' in them days.

When my Dad was in his mid-sixties, he was also diagnosed with emphysema which made me realise that I didn't actually know how my Grandad had died. When I asked my Dad, he told me that his Dad was forever coughing and one day he had a bad coughing fit, sucked in hard to get a lung full of air but his dentures shot down his throat instead of the air, then he couldn't breathe, so he died. I have got a vivid imagination and a terribly sick sense of humour so, although I knew that was an horrific way to snuff it, I had to let out a little laugh. It may have been the way that my Dad had told the story, so matter of fact like, I don't know but I just found humour in it. My Dad proper told me off and rightly so. When my Dad's emphysema proper kicked in during the last few years of his life, every time he had a coughing fit my Mum would say 'Take your teeth out Henry, you don't want to go the same way as your father', and then she'd laugh, so it wasn't only me that thought it was amusing.

My Mum's family were not at all like my Dad's; they were a bit more upper-class. My Nan kept the home immaculate as well as taking good care of her six kids and husband. She used to be a great cook and was very organised. As if all that wasn't enough, get this, she also worked as a cleaner at Waterloo station three nights a week to bring some more money in; what an absolute star! She had lots of siblings, but my absolute favourite was one of her younger sisters, the late and great 'Dolly'. When I first saw Catherine Tate's 'Nan' character on the telly, I cried laughing because she was so much like my great-aunt Dolly; not to look at because Dolly was always dressed beautifully in expensive and stylish clothes, but she sounded just like her. It was a proper shock when she opened her mouth because she looked so glamorous and posh. My Nan looked more like Catherine Tate's Nan, but she would never have spoken like that and she would often get embarrassed of what came out of her little sister's gob!

Dolly loved talking about her neighbour and would say, 'My neighbour is the salt of the earth and she's so generous, if she could shit through her ribs, she'd give her fucking arsehole away.' Priceless! On a good day, she could even get a profanity in the middle of a word; I thought that was pretty clever and fan-fucking-tastic! Dolly's daughter thinks that I am like her Mum; I shouldn't fucking think so!!

My Grandad was a policeman and a boxer. He had the most magnificent cauliflower ear and looked a right hard bastard, which he was. Right up until he died, he used to talk about the day he'd shaken hands with his hero, Muhammad Ali. He would point to his own right hand and say, 'This is the hand, that shook the hand, of the hand that shook the world'. I fucking love that line and it's very clever I think. I really loved my Grandad but looking back, he was a bit of a git really. He used to give my Nan the odd dig, which was a common pastime for men in them days but that sure as shit don't make it right! I always say that my Dad's family were a lower class than my Mum's, but there was never any tales of domestic violence with my Dad's lot and they didn't have any Tourette's Syndrome Sufferers either. I believe that my Mum's family had two of them. Dolly definitely suffered from Tourette's and I think my Grandad did too. Neither of them would have been diagnosed because it didn't have a name back then. My Grandad used to randomly shout out 'PRAT' or 'QUIM'. It didn't matter where he was or who he was with; if he got the urge, he'd open his gob and one, or both, of his favourite words would come bellowing out. 'Prat' wasn't a name for a silly person years ago, it was a nickname for a noony, as was 'quim'

197

and still is of course. When he shouted these naughty words, everyone used to get embarrassed, but I thought it was great and proper funny, although it did get me into trouble once.

It was on a Monday morning and my schoolteacher asked her class of six-year-olds if any of us had learnt any new words over the weekend. I was so excited as my little fat arm shot up into the air. I was invited to waddle (I was a fat kid) to the front of the class, given a piece of chalk and told to write my newly discovered word, in big letters mind, on the blackboard. I proudly wrote 'QUIM' and explained that it was my Grandad's favourite word. Consequently, I was told off and went back to my seat. I was devastated. My parents were called up to the school and I think they got told off too.

The following year they had to go to the school again because every Monday, for several weeks on the trot, I had written a similar story in my 'What I did at the weekend' book. It was along the lines of 'We all went to the pub. Daddy got drunk.

Mummy and Daddy were shouting at each other because Daddy drives bad when he is drunk.' Oops! I couldn't see what all the fuss was about. I used to love the weekends, sitting in the entrance of various Working Men's Clubs with my little bottle of Coke with a paper straw in and as many packets of Golden Wonder cheese and onion crisps that I could eat, larking about with my big sister and all of the other abandoned kids. We were as happy as pigs in shit and had a good old laugh.

When our parents took us to holiday camps, we used to be put to bed at night and left on our own while all the adults went to the club house to get on it. They never worried about us kids because if one of us cried loud enough (a petrified quiet sob wouldn't of been any good) a total stranger would come into our caravan or chalet, try to calm us down but if this was unsuccessful, he or she would walk to the club house and announce on a microphone something like 'There's a child crying in chalet number twenty.' Just think those strangers, that were employed by the holiday camp, could have been paedos, but nobody ever seemed to think about that then. That was the 1970's for ya!

My Mum was the apple of her Dad's eye. She was his princess and was still a virgin at the age of twenty-three when she met my Dad. She'd had loads of boyfriends; she was a proper stunner and had even done some modelling but was saving herself for someone special. Unlike her friend Joan who was known as a slut, simply because she used to let the boys 'French kiss' her, dirty cow, shocking behaviour! When my Dad asked my Grandad for my Mum's hand in marriage, he agreed but said he wasn't at all happy about it. On the morning of my parent's wedding, my Grandad said to my twenty-four-year-old virgin Mum, 'I think that you must be a sex-maniac. You are only marrying Henry because you can't wait to get at it.' Better still, she fell pregnant for the first time when she was thirty and he reacted to the good news by saying 'Oh great, I suppose you are going to start bashing them out every year now.' He was a bit of a hypocrite really because he'd had six kids by the time he was thirty; funny old bugger my Grandad.

My Mum got pregnant in October 1959 and had terrible morning sickness. She was offered a new drug that, she was told, would stop her vomiting morning, noon and night. She declined the offer because she was a 'fattist' and was happy to keep chucking up. She thought it would stop her from getting too fat during her pregnancy, how vain is that? She was a pregnant bulimic really. Thank goodness she was mind you, because those pills that she had been offered were the Thalidomide drug!

I used to live in a small bungalow opposite a woman who was a victim of that terrible drug. I'm normally a compassionate person but this bird pushed me to the limit, she was a nasty piece of work and one devious, crafty little bastard. Perhaps I shouldn't say 'little' coz that's pretty obvious because she didn't have any legs. That seems heartless, but not as heartless as she was and perhaps I shouldn't have nicknamed her 'Leggy' either, because that seems cruel, but it ain't as cruel as she was. I first saw her the day after I'd moved into my bungalow. I got home from work and she was in her front garden screaming, crying and waving her hands in the air. I ran over to her because I thought she'd fell into a hole and hurt herself. When I got to her she started laughing and said, 'I'm not in a hole, I haven't got legs'. She thought that was funny in some way; I didn't. She went on to explain that she pulled that stunt all the time because she liked seeing people's frightened faces. Nice. Now, in normal circumstances, I would have given her a mouthful, but I let it go.

What I didn't let go in the months to follow, however, was how she took the piss out of two of our neighbours; one who had learning difficulties, a man in his fifties with the mental age of twelve and an elderly lady, who lived next door to her. Until I got involved, she used to ponce money off them both, daily, and used them like they were her staff. Her bungalow was so dirty that you could smell it from the outside. She had carers but if they were people of colour, she'd tell them to 'Fuck off', so she was racist too. Thankfully, the authorities took my complaints seriously and eventually moved her into residential care to be looked after by professionals and to stop her robbing vulnerable neighbours. Good riddance Leggy!

Chapter 7 I travelled with Gavin, I split up with Gavin

I had never met my Aussie aunt before, so when Gavin suggested that we go to Australia I was delighted. I gave in my notice at work and we booked the flights. Gavin wasn't working at the time; he often wasn't because he was more than okay for money. He got regular interest from a lump sum of money he had inherited when his brother had died and I think his parents treated him quite often, so he flew out first. I missed him so much in those couple of weeks that we were apart, but we emailed each other every day and he kept me posted on his adventures. Perhaps I should have left when he did really, but I did have stuff to sort out and I have always had a strong work ethic and wanted to honour my notice period; what a mug!

I flew into Perth airport and Gavin was there to collect me. He was holding a sign in front of him which said, 'Welcome to Australia Tig-Pig'. He looked great and his suntanned face had a huge childlike grin on it. What a wonderful moment, it was like something out of a film. He picked me up, spun me around and then we had a snog. I hate public signs of affection, but I made an exception in this case. Gavin had stayed in a couple of hostels in the two weeks that we had been apart, but the one he was living in then was a corker. It's the people that are staying in a hostel that makes it good or bad, not the facilities; just as well because this one was a bit of a dump really. There was a fantastic group staying there; characters from all over the world. I fitted in with his new friends perfectly and Gavin and I became like a 1970's double-act, we loved entertaining our new audience.

He had got a job at the hostel, running residents to and from the airport in a little minibus, but I became a lady of leisure for the first time ever. The only time I hadn't worked in the past was when I was ill and that doesn't count. Now I was healthy, temporarily retired and enjoying it lots. We had parties every night and loads of water fights to cool us down in the forty-five-degree heat. Our favourite restaurant was a Chinese named 'The Golden Shower'. We thought that was just the funniest name ever, but the owners obviously didn't realise that they had named their place after the kinky sex act where people pissed on each other to get their strange kicks. We stayed at that hostel for many weeks and met an abundance of strange, but fun-loving people and we were still there on Christmas Day. What a mad day that was. We had a barbecue for dinner and then went for a swim and a sunbathe on nearby Cottesloe beach. A few weeks before, some poor sod had gone for his early morning swim in the sea at Cottesloe and a shark had bitten his leg off. It was tragic because he could have survived but there was nobody about to help him, so, I'm sorry to say, he had bled to death on the beach. I know it's crazy, but we still swam in the sea on Christmas Day. I think you have a different mindset when you're away from home.

After Christmas dinner and our swim, we had yet another water fight at the hostel followed by a boozy but chill-some evening; it was wonderful. New Year's Eve was just as good. We saw the New Year in but then decided it would be a great idea, probably due to the amount of alcohol that we had in us, to stay awake until 8am because that was the start of the new year in the UK. Silly really because at 11am we boarded a train to go to Adelaide.

When I told Gavin that I hoped it wasn't going to be a long train journey, he showed me the distance between Perth and Adelaide on the map and it was only inches away, so no problem! He had got us the cheapest train tickets available and I noticed that our carriage didn't look dissimilar to the ones that ran between Shoeburyness and Fenchurch Street back at home. It had high-backed, dirty, hard seats with dried-up chewing gum and head sweat, from thousands of previous passengers, embedded into them and there was very little leg room. We were sat opposite two lads from Southend, which is only twelve miles from Basildon, what were the chances of that?! They proudly showed us the ten giant spliffs, banged out with cannabis, that they had prepared for the hellishly long journey. 'Long journey?' I said, 'Yes' the lads replied, 'We won't get into Adelaide for another forty-three hours.' Gavin had now turned his head away from me and was looking out the window, desperately trying not to laugh. I shouted, 'For fuck's sake Gavin, when was you gonna tell me that I have got to sit in this uncomfortable chair for forty-three hours looking out of the window with nothing to see apart from the Nullarbor, seriously?'. The Nullarbor is an endless desert, no trees, no buildings, no people or any sign of life apart from the odd kangaroo and most of them that we saw were dead; they probably had died from sheer boredom. Oh well, that's the way it is, best we get stoned off our tits to pass the time, giggle uncontrollably and talk utter bollocks with the lads until we get there. Our main cause of hysterical laughter was the girl that was sitting a bit further down the carriage from us. She was amazing, no lie, she snored very loudly and grunted like a pig for almost forty hours of that journey. She had her mouth open, was dribbling and did the odd fart; a bit like me in normal circumstances really.

When we finally arrived in Adelaide, we all headed for the nearest YHA. These were the most expensive hostels, but they were much classier, with really comfy bunk beds and we all needed a good night's sleep after being awake for more than two days! Gavin and the lads checked in an all-male dormitory and me, into a female one. There was only one bed free in my dorm, a top bunk, so I climbed up and shut my tired eyes. Then I heard a familiar sound, it couldn't be? Oh yes, it fucking could be! I leant over and looked at the bunk below me and there she was, the 'sleep-monster' from the train. Hadn't she had enough fucking sleep on the journey? Her snoring didn't seem so funny now in my non-stoned and sleep-deprived state I can tell you. How's me luck?! It took me ages to get to sleep because of that noisy cow, but I did manage, eventually, to go into a sleeping coma.

We went to visit my Aunt Becky the next day, who had lived in Adelaide since she'd emigrated. She had long since been divorced and her two kids, Sarah and Steven, had left home. Sarah was now living in Canada with her long-term partner and their two children, so there was no chance of us meeting them sadly. Steven was with his partner and their three children in an amazing town called Warburton, which was a long way away from Adelaide, on the outskirts of Melbourne.

Becky was meeting us at the coach station. She lived an hour drive away from the city centre so we had decided to get a coach, so she wouldn't have to drive too far to get us. I was feeling a bit nervous because I had never met her before and I was hoping we would get on and that her house was okay, because we had arranged for us to stay with her for a few days. When the coach pulled in, there was a massive crowd waiting to collect people from the many coaches that were arriving. 'What does your Aunt look like?' Gavin said, 'I ain't got a clue, I've never met the woman' I replied. Then a bit of panic set in because she didn't know what I looked like either. However, I immediately spotted her beautiful little head amongst the sea of faces. She looked just like my Dad and my other six aunties. All my Dad's family are very good-looking and ridiculously small; they would all fit in a treat in the 'Land of Oz'....see what I did there? There was an instant family love bond between Becky and I, probably because she was as scatty and as wonderfully eccentric as the rest of her siblings. We had the best few days with her, she was the perfect hostess and we enjoyed meeting some of her sailing friends too. They told us that Becky was a very good yachtswoman due to the fact that she was slim, fit and agile, which is the perfect combo to be a good sailor apparently. Thanks to Becky, I saw my first Redback spider that lived happily at the end of her garden; nasty fucking things they are! She drove us to so many spectacular places including the harbour where, a couple of times a week, literally tens of thousands of jellyfish come to have a little look around the boats; it was an amazing sight. I also loved hearing all of her stories about my Dad and her sisters, from when they were kids growing up in Dagenham, and about the things that had happened to her since she had moved to Australia; some were good things and some, seriously, not so good. Her divorce story was mental and made mine sound quite pathetic by comparison.

At the end of our stay with Becky, she drove us back to the city centre where we met up with the Southend lads again. They had hired a car and were going up into the Adelaide hills for a few nights to stay in a caravan and invited us along. I can't remember much about that trip because I was stoned for most of it, but I do remember how beautiful the mountains were and I saw my first Aussie snake and Huntsman spider. The Huntsman is one big spider, but it can't hurt you they say. Oh yes it fucking can because if I woke up with one of those giant fuckers on my face I would have a heart attack and die! From Adelaide we went to Melbourne, which I really liked but Gavin wasn't too keen, so we moved on. I was gutted that I never got to see my cousin

Steven, but I had already decided that this was not going to be my only visit to Australia, so I would meet him on my next trip. Next was Canberra, Sydney and then basically up to the top, into the middle and out again and back to where we'd started, in Perth. It took us over a year, but we managed to see lots of Australia and spent several weeks in New Zealand as well, which was great. We then headed back home; all good things must come to an end and all that bollocks.

It was so nice to see our families and friends again. I had missed my lot so much that, at times, it used to hurt my heart and turn me into a blubbering mess. That couldn't have been a pretty sight because I have been told, by numerous people, that I have got the ugliest 'cry-face' ever. We were only back in the UK for two months, but it was wonderful to spend Christmas at home with our loved ones and to see the new millennium in.

We then buggered off again, this time to South-East Asia. We flew to Singapore and both liked it there, but it was well expensive. If we had stayed there for more than a week, all of our money would have been gone so we got a third class train ticket, that's the cheapest one there is, to check Malaysia out. There was no glass in the windows in third class, so it was a bit breezy and very noisy. The loos were something else; someone had got a blunt jigsaw and cut out a round hole in the floor of the small toilet cubicle, so you could see the railway tracks whizzing past below you just inches away and on the wall there was a tap with a proper manky old bit of hosepipe attached to it. You had to remove your lower garments, squat over the hole, do your business onto the tracks, hose your private parts down and that's ya lot. I used to feel amazingly clean after a visit to the loo, even though there wasn't a bit of bog-roll in sight. It is a bit of an artform though because the trains are very old and shaky, so you need to get your aim right, but I cracked it. What I didn't like was the walk back to my seat after vacating the toilet because there was so much gob on the aisle floor and I was frightened that I would go arse-over-tit and land in it! A lot of Asians do like a good spit, but they don't want to chance spitting out of the open windows, due to the high possibility of a splashback, so the aisle is the only other place for them to empty the contents of their lungs. Not nice, but it is what it is.

I was fascinated by the cleverness of the giant spiders outside, that there were literally hundreds of. They spun their webs in between the wires of the very high telegraph poles; what a great idea. They obviously got loads to eat because they were humongous. Sometimes the webs seemed a bit too close to the train and I had visions of one of the monstrous creatures launching themselves with their webs, like they had been SAS trained, into the carriage and onto my face. It used to make my bum-hole go a bit tight, I can tell you.

On that journey I noticed, that in the many towns that we passed through, how happy everyone looked, even though their accommodation was terrible. They lived in badly made huts mainly and the water in the never-ending stream, that seemed to

215

follow us the whole way, was filthy. We assumed they drank from that water and bathed in it. However, they all looked so clean, healthy and happy; very different to the often-miserable faces you see in most, so called, rich countries. Another lesson learned.

We visited five South-East Asian countries over the next ten months and always travelled third class and lapped up the chaos, the atmosphere and the total madness of our train journeys. It made us feel as though we were a million miles away from home and we loved that feeling. It was quite late when we got to Malaysia. Our train pulled into Kuala Lumpur station and we spotted a hostel that was just by the exit of the train station. Gavin said, 'That will do us, let's get some sleep and we'll explore in the morning'. It turned out to be the worst place that either of us had ever stayed in. The reception on the ground floor seemed okay and it was very cheap to stay there, but when we got upstairs it was ridiculously bad. There was just one dorm with six bunk beds in, which were all occupied except for our one. The other residents all looked fucking scary. People do tend to stare at you in Asia, but they're not being rude, bogging you out all aggro like, they are simply being nosey. This lot, however, were bogging us out, they all looked like proper wrong-uns. Gavin said, 'Don't make eye contact with anyone and let's just get into bed.' He insisted that we slept side-by-side on the lower bunk; me against the wall, for safety reasons, but that turned out to be a nightmare because it was baking hot and the humidity was unbearable. The bed felt wet when we laid on it, but it didn't really matter because we were both sweating buckets so it would have gotten wet soon enough anyway, so whatever. I'm not sure if we fell asleep or passed out, but we went out like a light either way.

The next morning, seriously, the weirdos were in the same positions as they had been the night before and still staring at us. It bloody stunk in there too; I bet they'd had a 'fart-off' when we were asleep, dirty bastards. When I first opened my eyes, on that hellish morning, there were two fucking great big cockroaches on the wall that were about an inch from my face. Now normally I would have screamed, jumped out of bed and run around the dorm doing jazz hands, but I just released a tiny squeak and pointed them out to Gavin. He quickly pealed his soaking wet clothes off mine and said that we should take our rucksacks to the bathroom, freshen-up a bit and then just get out of there.

Much to our horror there was only one bathroom, which is ridiculous for twelve people. It was a wet room with a shower and an Asian toilet. This would have been fine, but the toilet and shower were both clogged up and obviously had been for several days. To get into the wet room, you had to step over the ledge and put your feet into shit that was ankle deep, oh yeah, actual watered-down by the shower 'shit'. We were both desperate to pee so in we went, one at a time, so the other one could make sure our bags weren't nicked. It was beyond disgusting and we left that hostel looking great! We both had other people's crap on our feet, sodden with sweat and stinking to high heaven. To add insult to injury, we walked two minutes up the road and saw a really nice hostel that had their 'vacancy' sign up!

We spent a month or so in Malaysia, including a visit to an island called 'Langkawi' that was like paradise. I've got a lovely photo of Gavin there, laying in a hammock, just looking out to sea. It was so relaxing, living in our little bamboo hut on the beach, that we didn't ever want to leave. The moonlight used to shine through the bamboo and give the illusion of a hundred stars scattered all around the hut; it was magical. We had a rare romantic moment there, whilst having dinner in a restaurant that was on the beach. It was just before sunset when we were shown to our table that was near the water's edge. After watching the sun melt into the calm, clear sea, we actually held hands while we waited for our food to arrive. We had the most wonderful candlelit meal but suddenly I got a terrible pain in my famously bad guts. 'Here we go again', I thought. Thank fuck I had a very long, flowy dress on because as I stood up, the poo came gushing down! Gavin was excellent, he said 'Don't panic Tig, just go back to the hut and sort yourself out'. I tried to look casual as I quickly walked away. As I looked back, there he was, love him, discreetly kicking sand over the unwanted tip I'd left behind, while getting the waiter's attention to pay the bill. Nightmare. Apart from that, we had a wonderful evening. Of course, we had to leave that paradise island eventually so, a few days later, we got back on the train to Thailand.

My first impressions of Thailand were not too good. When we got off the train, there was a big, badly handwritten sign saying, 'IF YOU TAKE DRUGS INTO THAILAND YOU WILL BE SHOT.' All righty then, welcome to Thailand! Our train had travelled through the night, so we had taken turns in sleeping because, at the time, it was common practice for local drug dealers to put their gear into unsuspecting tourist's bags. They would then let them get it through customs, if they were lucky, then the scumbags would mug them to get the drugs back, nice! We went to Bangkok for a couple of days, which was as mad as we had been told it would be and then started to travel about. We went to a few of the islands; Koh Phi Phi, Phuket and the lovely Koh Lanta but then headed to the non-tourist destination of Chumphon, to visit Gavin's friend John. I loved John; he was a big fat bald bloke and Gavin's only friend that hadn't been to public school. He was a builder and a proper down to earth geezer, unlike the other lot. Him and Gavin had backpacked in Thailand years before and John had met a local girl there, fell in love and had never returned to the UK again. His girlfriend, Pong, couldn't speak hardly any English and me, not a word of Thai, but we managed to communicate just fine, how mad is that. Just as well really because we stayed with them for a good few months. I really enjoyed their company and they were great hosts. We all got on very well and used to have a right laugh. Pong would often try to get her little arms around John and say 'He so fat' which used to make us roll up. She thought his large frame was very sexy because fat Thai blokes often became sumo wrestlers and they were heartthrobs in Thailand. It was nice living in an unspoilt bit of the country and I really enjoyed going out on our mopeds to explore every day. It also made a nice change to go into a restaurant without having to endure seeing young, sometimes very young, Thai girls up on a stage with different colour garlands around their necks, waiting to be hired for the night by some fat old British man, fucking perverts!

Apart from Chumphon, I found Thailand very upsetting. The scenery was always beautiful, in fact it's pretty much the same all over South East Asia, but it was very apparent that there was no educational system in place in Thailand so the only way those poor girls could earn a living was prostitution. It's heart-breaking to witness. We were all upset when we finally said goodbye to John and Pong. I had taught her some more English and my Thai, thanks to Pong, was now basic but okay and off we went again.

John set-up an email address for Pong to enable us to keep in touch. It contained the word 'pongydraws' which John thought was well funny, stating 'She don't realise that means she stinks!'. A few years later they started a family and now have two children and are still happily living in Thailand. Gavin and I spent the next few months in Vietnam, which is home to the most wonderfully crazy people and lastly, we did Cambodia. We had some good times there, but we made the mistake of going on a tour and one of the stops was at the 'Killing Tree'. I'd never heard of it and wish I never had to be honest. It was a tree that was used during the War but there is no need for me to tell you about it, if you don't already know; let's just say that humans can be evil fuckers! Enough said.

When we returned home, we had an eventful five months before we went travelling again. Firstly, my flat had been sitting empty for a long time. I had bought it and hardly ever lived there. My Mum and Dad had lived in their house for forty odd years and, apart from their short time in Battersea when they'd first got married, this had been their only home and had a lifetime of memories, including me being born in the front bedroom. My Mum used to say that she and my Dad had always hoped to have been carried out of that house in a box one day, preferably at the age of ninety-seven! Unfortunately, my Dad's health was getting worse and he was having terrible trouble with the stairs. Consequently, when we got back, they asked me if I would mind if they sold the house and went to live in my flat, just until they found a suitable bungalow to buy. Sounded like a great idea because we had already decided to go to Spain the following June, to work and live for a year or so. The day they moved out of that house was one of the saddest days that any of us had ever had. I know you take the memories with you when you move and its only bricks and mortar and all that, but it was heart wrenching saying goodbye to that place. They actually loved living in my flat, so much so, that they lived there for another six years before they got a nice downstairs flat in a warden-controlled place where they happily lived, for their remaining years. All's well that ends well and all that bollocks!

The second event was that Gavin and I had discussed the possibility of becoming parents. Neither of us had ever fancied having children, but we thought we would be a great Mum and Dad so looked into IVF. I had, in the past, had so many problems in the womb area; cancer twice, polyps, fibroids and had five unsuccessful pregnancies. Please don't feel sad about the miscarriages because not one single one of the pregnancies had been planned. They were all more a case of 'fuck it, I am up the duff' scenarios. I had been told that after the various treatments I'd had over the years, that the only way I could possibly conceive would be with the help of IVF. Gavin said that if it didn't work, we would look into adoption after the Spanish adventure. Rightly so, Gavin couldn't understand why everyone wanted to make their own babies when there were so many children, who had already been born, that desperately needed a loving home so, adoption was a great plan 'B'.

Oh my days, 'the IVF month', as we later named it, was hysterical. I do realise that it's not supposed to be funny and, more often than not, it's a very stressful experience, but ours really was funny. For a start we had to go to Barts in London for all the treatment because that, and the sister hospital, the Royal London in Whitechapel, were the ones that had saved my life, twice, with the cancer business. Gavin didn't have the privilege of taking his sperm samples to a nearby doctors' surgery, oh no, he had to knock one out in a small room in the hospital. I couldn't have the daily injections in my bum at my GP's either, Gavin had to do them for me at home. He hated it and was so frightened that he would do it wrong and kill me. I wasn't thrilled about cocking my naked arse up into Gavin's face every morning and having a needle put in my butt cheek either, but how we laughed.

On the day when I was due to have the eggs removed and for Gavin to give up some more sperm, things didn't go to plan. For a start there was only the one 'wank room' which meant that me, Gavin and four other couples had to sit in the waiting room trying not to make eye contact whilst, one at a time, the men, when their names were called, had to go in and 'choke the chicken'. I'm sure things are different now, but that was the score then. The first bloke was called and went into 'the room.' Gavin looked at his watch and told me that he was gonna time him, to see what his competition was. Men eh, everything has to be a competition, even a five-knuckle-shuffle. After a while, the first bloke came back into the waiting room looking all red and embarrassed. He sat down next to his partner, who was equally as red-faced and couldn't even look at him and then they were taken off somewhere. The next one was called so Gavin looked at his watch again and informed me that the time to beat, so far, was nine minutes and forty-two seconds. 'Seriously Gavin, have a word with yourself' I said, although I must admit that his antics were giving me a huge ball of giggle build-up in my tummy. I was hoping Gavin would be third, but of course he was last. When Gavin eventually went into the room, he had got me at it because I looked at my watch. After twenty minutes I was getting a bit worried. He then appeared and told me that when his willy exploded, he'd panicked and pushed the test-tube so hard down onto it, that his helmet had got stuck and a nurse had to help him prise it off. That ball of giggle came out alright then, even Gavin had to laugh.

It was now time for eggs to meet the sperm, but something mad happened to me. I suddenly thought, 'This could actually work, we could have a baby, we won't be able to travel anymore apart from normal two week holidays, I will worry about the kid every day for the rest of my life, I would have sleepless nights thinking about cot death, I would have to do school runs and make small talk with the other Mums, I would have to worry about them being bullied at school, I would be so hurt if they got their heart broken and they die in their car after having passed their driving test'. Then I stopped thinking and said, 'What the fuck are we doing Gavin? I am so sorry, but I don't want to do this'. He didn't look at all shocked, bless him, he just casually said 'Tig, I wish you had told me that half an hour ago, before I entered the wank room'. He cuddled me and we both agreed that we had given in to the voices in our heads, that every human and every creature must have to prevent extinction, that tell us that we 'must' reproduce our species. We decided that we would seriously think about adoption in the future, but first our Spanish adventure was calling!

We started in Barcelona; plan being that we would backpack all the way up the Spanish coast looking for work, but if we hadn't got a job by the time we got to Portugal, we'd go and visit his Dad in his mansion in the Portuguese hills and then go back to the UK and adopt babies. We both absolutely loved Barcelona, but Gavin had very little chance of showing off his Spanish there, which he spoke very well, because the main language is Catalan which he couldn't speak a word of, so we moved on. Every place we went, there seemed to be no chance of getting work, which I was secretly pleased about because I was hoping that Benidorm would be where we ended up. I like Benidorm because it does what it says on the tin. I appreciate that most of the holidaymakers that go to the main town are drunken, disrespectful arseholes but the old town is wonderful because you feel like you are in Spain and not on a night out on the piss in England. The beaches are very clean, apart from first thing in the morning when there are always several Brits that have overdone it the night before, forgotten where their hotel was and had passed out by the sea. The sea is so clean and you can see right to the bottom, however far out you go and there are often shoals of fish to be seen too. When we got to Beni I was gutted because Gavin hated everything about the place, so that was that. We were having a great time in Spain but were beginning to get a bit disheartened on the job front.

When we arrived in Fuengirola, we went for a coffee and there was a local paper on the table. Gavin was half-heartedly flicking through it when he spotted an advert for a couple needed to run a bar. We didn't bother calling the number, we just went to have a look. The main part of Fuengirola has got a bit of the Benidorm about it, but when we walked along the seafront to where the bar was, we noticed that we seemed to be walking away from the chaos and into a much quieter and classier part of the town. It was like the walk from Southend into Shoeburyness, back in Essex. When we got to the bar it was shut and a sign in the window stated that it opened from 6pm until late. We went to find somewhere to stay and returned later that night. We met the owners, Pat and Paul, two older blokes that were originally from London and we all got on very well. They had owned the bar for many years but only ever opened in the evenings. The town had got a lot more popular in recent years, so they wanted to try opening during the daytime. Their plan was to employ a couple to start work at 8am to tidy up and restock from the night before and then open for breakfast at 10am, followed by a lunch menu to start at 1pm, they would then get to the bar at 6pm and take over. It sounded perfect and thankfully they thought we would be the ideal couple to try out their new venture. They offered us a generous salary and they recommended that we went to view a flat that had recently had a make-over and was only a ten-minute walk from the bar. OMG, it was too good to be true!

We started work a couple of days later. Our new bosses thought it was best that I did the cooking and Gavin was the face of the bar; that was obviously because he was funnier than me! I ain't the best cook in the world, especially when I'm stood behind a bar with my back to the customers, my face-sweat dripping onto the hotplate that I cooked everything on and standing in a pool of my own sweat but I did alright. The bar was quite an expensive place but all the food we served was good quality stuff. There was a bar next door that would have fitted in a treat in Benidorm; they were as cheap as chips and served chips with everything!

Pat and Paul said that they refused to serve chips or beans because that wasn't the type of clientele they wanted to attract. They were snobs really but that suited us just fine. Our bar was on the seafront and had lots of tables outside, but we were under strict instructions that if any low-life Brits sat down, Gavin was to go and greet them and inform them straightaway that if they wanted chips or beans it might be best if they went next door. Pat and Paul knew their stuff because it always worked; the lower-class people would get up and bugger off next door. Most of our customers were either Spanish or Brits that actually lived in Fuengirola, but we were always busy; it was very hard work, but we enjoyed it. We got Sunday afternoons off and every Monday because the bar shut for just that one day a week. Our two-bedroom apartment was beautiful. It was big, had a sea view, was very modern and it was in a nice quiet location. Life had never been better, and we were earning well, especially with the added bonus of tips.

Loads of our family and friends came to visit us when we were there, which we loved. We would leave our guests in bed in the morning to enable them to have a well-earned holiday lay-in and go off to work. When they were up and dressed, they'd come to the bar to have some breakfast and then go and spend the day on the beach or go sightseeing, perfect. They would join us when we had finished our shift and we'd all go out for dinner and on the lash. Happy fucking days!

One of our first visitors were Burt and Liz; he was my sisters first husband and the father of my eldest two nieces and she is his wife. They didn't have the best journey to get to us because they flew on the day that the Twin Towers were hit. Gavin actually told me off that day because he thought I'd turned the channel over on the TV in the bar, which I hadn't. He liked to have the news on during the day and he'd glanced at the screen and thought there was some disaster movie on. It was certainly a disaster, but not a movie unfortunately. We had shitloads more visitors but the ones that loved it the most were my parents who came for a week but stayed for six! Pat, Paul and Gavin were all so understanding regarding my homesickness. They covered for me every six weeks so I could go and visit my family back home.

Every so often, on a Sunday afternoon, Gavin and I would drive to Portugal and stay at Gavin's Dad and step-mum's place for the night. They were a funny old pair they were. His Dad's name was Stanley or 'Staners' as she called him, and her name was Jessica (the secretary) but he called her 'Jessiekins'. Yeah, what fucking ever! Their house was spectacular but a bit out in the sticks. It was massive, had two acres of land and a nice big swimming pool. They were ever-so, ever-so posh and swanned about like the Lord and Lady of the Manor. They must have asked me a hundred times to please not call them 'Stan' and 'Jess', but I just couldn't help myself; they brought out the naughty side in me. However, they did used to proper piss me off because that could not accept that Gavin and I were enjoying

Spain and had never been happier. They were fucking obsessed with him 'doing better for himself'. We were happy, healthy and loving life; what more could they want for Gavin? On my birthday they were super-excited about giving me my pressie. They had found a place in Fuengirola that did elocution lessons and thought I would benefit from the course tremendously. Oh really! I just wanted to say, 'Go fuck yourselves' when I opened the envelope containing the voucher for my ten lessons, but this was my boyfriend's Dad and step mum, so at first, I just thanked them. After a few minutes I realised that I wasn't able to calm myself down. I was proper angry and insulted, so I handed the envelope back to them and said that I was sorry, but I wasn't going to accept their gift and hoped that they could get their money back. They were genuinely shocked and said, 'You are an intelligent girl, but people assume that you are stupid, because of your accent.' Gavin said that my reply was perfect; I said 'I believe that anyone who gauges my level of intelligence because of my accent, is an idiot' and added 'I know you may both find this hard to understand, but I genuinely like my accent because it comes from my home town.' I really wanted to add, 'So stick that up ya pipe and fucking smoke it, you complete and utter snobs!!!!' but of course, I didn't.

The bar shut for a week at Christmas because that was when Pat and Paul' once-a-year visit to see their loved ones in the UK was. I obviously went to spend Christmas with my family, but Gavin had decided to spend his with Stan and Jess. Fuck knows what they said to him when he was there, perhaps they offered him a big wad of cash; I will never know but the new year was not a happy one. 'My' Gavin had disappeared, and I wasn't liking the new one much at all. His personality had fucked off. He was now so serious and quiet and, worst of all, our sex-life went from excellent to non-existent. Gavin was always tight with money, which didn't bother me, but being tight with his willy was a different 'ballgame'....see what I did there? Please don't think that I was some sort of sex maniac because I really wasn't. I would have been more than happy with just an occasional cuddle, but he had stopped 'all' physical contact with me, and I didn't get as much as a peck on the cheek anymore. The next couple of times that he went to visit his Dad, he asked if I'd mind if he went alone. This went on for a few months and I tried to talk to him about it but was getting nothing back. I tried everything to seduce him too, but again, nothing. Finally, he told me that he'd managed to enrol on a course back in the UK, to become a counsellor. He asked me to return home with him but said that he would understand if I wanted to stay in Spain. I couldn't let him go that easily because I truly loved the 'original' Gavin. He flew back home just days after his announcement, but I stayed working at the bar for another couple of weeks, until Pat and Paul had employed a replacement couple. I was so proper gutted to leave that life.

We had worked in that wonderful bar for fifteen months, but I would happily of stayed there for much longer. Back in the UK,

Gavin had rented a house for us just outside of Basildon. It was nice but certainly not as nice as our flat in Spain. The 'no-sex or cuddles' thing carried on and Gavin was just constantly studying, in total silence. Two months I lived in that house but got sick of trying to get close to him. When I tried to talk to him about how unhappy I was and how I thought that he was suffering from some sort of depression, he would actually shout at me, which 'my' Gavin would never have done. Eventually, as heart-breaking as it was, I did what I had to do and left him.

I never saw or spoke to Gavin again. Six years after I had moved out of that house, I received a phone call informing me that Gavin had died. He hadn't been suffering from any kind of illness; he just went to bed one night and never woke up. They'd put it down to 'adult cot death' because the post-mortem showed no medical reason why he had died. He was thirty-six years old. Stanley and Jessica asked me to attend the funeral because I was the only woman that Gavin had ever lived with. They also requested that I brought some photographs along of our many travels together because they didn't have any. My friends, Burt and Liz, had stayed in contact with Gavin after we had split-up and they kindly offered to take me to the funeral. We didn't go to the 'do' after the church service, but I did give Stanley a nice big stack of photos. Gavin was buried on top of his brother, Simon, and the two brothers now share a headstone. Stanley spoke at the funeral and said that because Gavin had been taken from us so young, he was now glad that he had spent many years travelling. It was a bit late to approve of his lifestyle now, but fair play to the old boy for saying it. The last six years of Gavin's life were very different to his earlier years. He had studied hard and became a counsellor, but he didn't enjoy that, so he started to study again; this time to become an architect but he died before he'd finished his degree. He had done no travelling since we had split-up and, from what his friends told me, he didn't laugh much and had lost his amazing lust for life. Tragic.

Chapter 8 I travelled alone, I met Brian

When I first moved out of mine and Gavin's house in Essex, I went to stay with my friend Lauren (who I had worked with in the mobile phone shop years before) for a week or so, until I found a house-share to live in. I loved living at Lauren's because she has a way of making everything seem okay and I proper needed that then. Without Lauren, and her beautiful inside-and out daughter Esther, I would have been in a terrible state. I wasn't great, but I held it together, most of the time. If Lauren had a three-bedroom house, I think I may never have left! My new house-share was okay, and I got myself a job and decided to try to live a normal life until my wounds were healed. Of course, my normal life was short-lived because I went, on my own, on a year-long globe-trotting adventure. I feel that I'm showing off now and giving it large, but I did see some wonderful places that year and met so many new people to entertain, solo this time! I went to China first, but only for a week on an organised sightseeing tour. I thought it would make me feel safer and get me back in to being a solo traveller, and it worked. I did the Beijing tourist attractions, but there are lots of those, so I had a busy and enjoyable week. I didn't realise that when people said they had 'climbed' The Great Wall of China, that they were talking literally. Some of it you do have to actually climb, well, in my case, crawl up on all fours and then slide down on my arse!

Then India, my favourite place in the world. I was only intending to be there for ten days but ended up having a two month stay! I hired a driver when I first arrived, just for the ten days, to take me around the Golden Triangle of Delhi, Agra and Jaipur, with many more stops en route. In New Delhi I told my driver that I had seen loads of Bollywood movies back at home, but had always wanted to see one in India, so he drove me to one of the many cinemas. He said that they all have male-only sections which are seated and comfortable, but the female sections are basically on ya bum on the floor, at the front. Thankfully, as he nicely pointed out, I looked like a man so would be able to be seated, providing I didn't speak and let him do the talking. Well, at least I still had a feminine voice I suppose so that was a bonus. For some reason, bugs and various other creatures like to make themselves at home in my usual mop of hair, so it had to go. I had my head shaved to a number two crop before setting off on my travels and I was thin, had no tits, thus, looked like a bloke. It was at the Taj Mahal that me and my driver really bonded, and our friendship began, because he was so chuffed that I appreciated and loved his country so much. He got us to the Taj very early in the morning, to enable me to see the sunrise there. I loved the place so much that I nagged him into letting me stay there until the sunset and this is how I got to meet his family. He didn't live far from there, so he went home for a few hours to see his wife and many children and returned after sunset, to collect me. Our next stop was miles away, so he suggested that I stayed with his family for the night and headed off in the morning. I was delighted; what an honour to stay in an Indian 'home' rather than a hotel. They lived in a small village and their house was actually a cave, but it was spotlessly clean and very welcoming. After the wife had cooked me a spectacular dinner, they showed me my bedroom; it was on the roof and I could see, in the distance, the Taj Mahal, incredible. I was in the open-air with just a tent type structure above me, which was covered by a mosquito net. WOW! I fucking loved it! The sky was full of stars, surely I had died and gone to heaven! In the morning, his wife and two of their children gave me a tour of their village. I was overwhelmed by their friendliness and the simplicity of their lifestyle.

I was gutted that we had to move on, but I still had so much to do and see. I'm glad I did finish the tour because I wouldn't have wanted to miss the thrill of being taken to the top of the Amber Palace in Jaipur on the back of an elephant for one; even though I was shitting myself. Fuck me, elephants are big! I could have got on another elephant to go back down too but feared for my life, so I opted to walk but ended up having a massive row with an American couple. In every Indian city that I had visited so far, I had witnessed the horror of children begging on the streets; even walking in between the traffic of the manic roads to tap on car windows or lean into tuk-tuks to beg and risking their lives every day. It was heart-breaking, as was the scene that I witnessed on my walk down from the Amber Palace. A local young woman was sitting on a rock, sobbing and desperately trying to feed her small baby from her breast, but the baby was dead. I asked my driver what we could do to help her, and he said that he would phone the authorities to report the terrible scene and someone would come to help her. I'm still not sure, to this day, if he was telling me the truth, but I like to think that he was. We were just about to continue our descent when, behind us, I heard what I thought was a camera clicking. When I looked over my shoulder, I saw an American couple taking photos of the distraught woman and her baby! I lost the plot; what the fuck were they going to do with those photographs, put them in an album to show their family and friends? Seriously, where was their respect and compassion, the sick bastards? When I said that I had a row, it wasn't really a row. I just gave the wankers the verbal beating that they deserved.

I was gutted when it was time for me to go off to Nepal because I was told that it was unsafe for me to travel there; it had all kicked off again. I was so disappointed when I received that news at the airport because I wasn't ready for the normality of Australia just yet. My driver, and now my friend, could see how choked I was so he said, 'You can come stay with me and my family for a while if you like?', I instantly replied, 'That'll do me, thank you very much.' I lived in the village and slept on the roof of the cave for nine fabulous weeks. I paid for my bed and board by giving English lessons so there is now a remote Indian village where the residents speak 'Basildon' and use English swear words quite a lot! I used to bathe in the stream, help cook on open fires, play lots of football with the local kids (geezer bird) and was barefoot for my entire stay. That was a piece of me living there surrounded by kind, easy-going, fun-loving and family-orientated people but I had to move on because my visa was due to expire and then I would have been breaking the law.

Australia next to revisit my favourite bits, but firstly I wanted to finally meet my cousin Steven. When I did, it was a very similar scene to when I'd first met his Mum, my Aunt Becky, three years previously in Adelaide. Steven was there to welcome me when my coach pulled up in his hometown, Warburton in Victoria. This was even more emotional because he looked exactly how my Dad had done in his younger days. He was so dark and handsome, with an award-winning smile. It was love at first sight again, but this time between two long lost cousins. He was just as good a host as his Mum had been, which wasn't easy for the poor sod because a few weeks before I had arrived, he had been forced to move out of his family home where his, now, ex-partner was still living with their three children. You could say that my visit was bad timing, but I think I was a healthy distraction from what they were all going through. Steven and I lived in a mobile home type place during my two months in Warburton, which was great, apart from when I first walked into my new home. There was a Huntsman spider on the wall, behind my bed, so I said to Steven 'Deal with that please'. I meant for him to get a bucket, it was that big, scoop it up and walk it ten miles away from the mobile home but he misunderstood. Being born and brought up in Australia obviously gives you a different attitude towards spiders because he proceeded to bang the wall next to the spider and it fell behind my bed. He genuinely thought that I just didn't want to look at it and because it wasn't venomous, he assumed that I would be happy with 'out of sight, out of mind'. NOOOOOOOO!!!! It's a good job we got pissed that night because I wouldn't have slept a wink otherwise. Steven's children were adorable; he had Lucy, George and Leo. I spent a lot of time with his kids. The boys were still babies, but Lucy was seven years old and was such an amazing little girl. She was so intelligent, great fun to be around and a very gifted violinist and pianist. Warburton is a wonderful place. It's set in the Yarra Valley, surrounded by mountains and unspoiled beauty. I felt at home and very chilled there and loved being with my family, but again, it was time to move on.

I worked in many hostels as a cleaner or on reception during the next several months, all over Australia. I had a couple of romantic relationships during my travels and even became a lesbian for a while. 'Don't knock it 'til you've tried it' as they say! I actually went to Fiji with her, again, another beautiful part of our world and we stayed on three of the islands in total; each one was as welcoming as the next. There were no cars or electricity on those islands and the locals were all such lovely, simple, Godfearing people. I finished my trip by having a few days in Los Angeles and could see the famous 'Hollywood' sign from my bedroom window. I love the film 'Pretty Woman' and had always wanted to walk up and down outside the Regent Beverly

Wilshire hotel saying, 'Work it, work it, own it'. It's ridiculous really, but that's just the way I am, little things please little minds!

I was ready to come home. I was now thirty-nine years old and thought it was time to calm it down a bit and grow up. I started temping in various accounts departments and moved into another house-share. I was due to turn forty in the August and my friend Charlie, the one I tried to kill with my Chopper bike when I was fifteen, asked me if I would like to visit him and his male partner, in their home in Spain, as an early birthday treat. I went there in July, for what was supposed to be a week, but stayed until the following January. So much for calming it down! I have always loved Spain and Charlie and his wonderful partner Gary, or my Gary-pops, as I fondly call him. Gary is one funny fucker and brings out my mischievous side something terrible. Every evening that I stayed with them, I used to call Gary up to my bedroom after my shower and ask him to put after sun lotion on my back. He bloody hated doing it because I would stand with my back to him, with just a towel around my naked body, and wait for him to start putting the lotion onto my back (whilst he heaved continuously by the way) then I would drop my towel, turn my head to look at him with my little finger in the corner of my mouth and say, 'Oops, sorry.' He would then run out of my room, screaming and doing jazz hands, whilst shouting 'Charlie, Charlie, she's doing it again!!!!'. I never grew tired of doing that; it got funnier every time!

I moved into a house-share after a couple of weeks, just around the corner from Charlie and Gary's, and got myself a job in a local fish and chip restaurant. The owner was not nice to work for, so I left after a few weeks and got another job. This time I was working with Gary in a much nicer restaurant. I'm sure that half of our customers used to dine there just to hear mine and Gary-pops constant amusing banter. I was having a great time, but I felt guilty for staying in Spain for so long because, unbeknown to me, my family had organised a surprise party for my fortieth birthday; they cancelled it of course. I spent my fortieth with my Charlie, Gary and some bloke I was seeing at the time. I had the best birthday ever. They took me out for a traditional Spanish lunch, followed by an evening in my favourite bar where, on the stroke of midnight when I was officially forty years old, I sang Roy Orbison's classic hit 'It's over' very badly, on a karaoke machine. I ended the night by jumping, half-naked, into a swimming pool. The voices in my head kept telling me to 'grow up' but I wouldn't listen. When I returned to the UK I moved into, what turned out to be, my favourite house-share ever. I got a permanent job, which I liked, and met a bloke that I stayed with for the next ten years; see, I really had grown up!

In between husbands, I have lived in some funny old places, all over the world; there I go showing off again! I was once in a house-share that got struck by lightning when I was in bed and it burnt down, hence my fear of storms. Another, where I walked into the bathroom on my first morning to find the landlord soaping up his willy in the shower but turned down his offer to join him, mainly because he had LBS. I had one where the landlord suffered with obsessive compulsive disorder so badly that I used to hear him in the middle of the night, on his hands and knees, picking fluff off the carpet on the stairs and I used to have to use a tape measure to replace my toiletries on the shelf in the bathroom.

However, none of them compare to the last one that I lived in. Having finally returned from Spain, after seven fun-filled months, I found what turned out to be my final ever house-share accommodation. My parents were still living in my flat, so I was homeless again. There was a room to let advertised in the local newspaper that sounded ideal, so I called the number and had a chat with Dennis, the landlord. I was fully aware that he was interviewing me on the telephone because I had been a landlady in the past, so I knew what he was doing. I must have come across okay because he invited me to go look at the room. The house was huge, it had six bedrooms and Dennis and his wife had built a small bungalow in the massive garden, that they lived in. We went upstairs to see the room whilst chatting away and suddenly Dennis stopped, looked at me and said, 'Hang on, you're not English, are you?'. I thought he was sodding about, so I just laughed, but he went on to say, 'Seriously, we don't allow English people to live here.' Apparently, he had been renting the rooms of his house out for many years and the only trouble he'd ever had with his house guests, had been with 'the English' as he called us. He was a South African bloke and had mistakenly thought that I was Australian when he'd spoken to me on the phone. When I then explained to him that, because of my travels abroad and especially when I had run the Spanish bar with Gavin, that I made him right regarding his opinion of us English folk. It upsets me to say this but in every country that I've visited, it's almost guaranteed that any bad or disrespectful behaviour is done by the English; sad, but true. One of the many reasons that I love spending time in different countries is, I know for a fact, I have convinced lots of people that not all the English are bad. I believe that if you are abroad, you instantly become an ambassador for your country and should do your very best not to let your home country down, but not everyone gets that, more's the pity.

Dennis liked me and offered me the room, but he had to inform me about something before I agreed to take it. Him, his wife and his girlfriend (greedy bastard) were naturists. Again, I thought he was joking but no, he was only dressed at that moment because I was coming to see the room. He was a self-employed accountant and worked from home. His wife used to get the shopping in, and he rarely left the house or put clothes on. I asked if the other residents were also naturists and was told that the Chinese couple, the Irish lad and the Russian lady were not, but the Polish and Turkish couples were. Oh fuck it, as long as it wasn't compulsory for me to walk around with my old noony and bangers out, I was moving in. There was a large communal kitchen and a lounge, which had sofas, a TV and of course, like every good house-share should have in the middle of the lounge, a double waterbed!!!

When I told my parents about my new home, they thought it was hysterical and said it was only me that could get herself into these situations. They weren't shocked at all because they had known me to do much worse than move into the 'nudey-house' that my Mum called it. Years before, when I was married to Lenny, husband number two, I had been poorly and couldn't go out to work for a while, so I decided to work from home. Mine and Lenny's closest friends were Cliff and Donna and they knew somebody that earned lots of money by making sexy calls for an '0898' company. I thought, with me being an ex-actress, I would be good at that and I was quite right, I was a natural. I had the strangest telephone interview to get that job I can tell you and it's the only job that I've not mentioned on my CV! I was told that I had to create three different characters in my head and name them, but I couldn't have a name if one of the other workers were already using it. You see, they got a lot of regular customers that would phone the main number and ask to receive a phone call from say 'Dirty Doris' for example, at 3pm that day. Dirty Doris would phone the customer at the allotted time and make the call last between ten and fifteen minutes. She would get paid for the amount of minutes that she was on the phone, but only up to fifteen, and also get the cost of the phone call refunded, when she sent her itemised BT bill to her employers. Sounded good to me, but before I accepted my odd new job, I asked them if they had any advice for me about what to do or say during the calls. The only tip they gave me was to pretend that I was having an asthma attack if I got lost for words! Easy-peasy or what.

My characters had to have different genres; my dominatrix name was Mistress Mandy, my older and posher lady was Felicity and my sweet and innocent name was Bella; I actually wanted Kelly, however, that name had already been taken. I couldn't have taken the job if it'd been for one of those companies that insisted that I gave my landline number to the customers so they could phone me direct, because Shane and Harry lived with Lenny and I at the time. If Shane or our lovely Harry had picked up the phone and there had been a bloke at the end of the line knocking one out, they wouldn't have been best pleased; they both knew what I was doing to earn some extra cash and they thought it was very amusing but, rightly so, they didn't want to get involved. Quite often, the four of us would be downstairs watching TV and I would announce that I was going upstairs for twenty minutes to make one of my calls. I would sit on my bed, normally in my old terry towelling dressing gown, with a fag in my hand and phone the customer. More often than not, and regardless of which character they wanted to get a call from, they would start by asking what I looked like. If I'd have told them the truth, they would've had absolutely no chance whatsoever of getting aroused, so I used to lie. I could visualise what my characters would look like, but I found it easier to describe their appearance from a picture, so I cut out three photos from an Ann Summers catalogue that looked like how I saw them in my head. I did that job for months, found it easy money and never had to pretend that I was asthmatic. The strangest bloke I spoke to, and there were lots to choose from, was Mr Jones. I had to call him at 6pm every Friday, as Mistress Mandy, and repeat the same routine every time, at his request of course. I had to spend the first eight or nine minutes just verbally abusing him by saying that he was a disgusting pervert and not fit to walk the earth, blah blah. Then, because he had been such a naughty boy, I told him to get a pencil from his desk, sharpen it until the point was very sharp, pull his trousers down, get onto all fours, shove the pencil up his bum and bark like a dog. That done it, I used to hear a slight groan and he would hang-up the phone. I bet he was a bloke in his fifties, bald, fat, suited and booted and the owner of a successful company with his own office; that hopefully had blinds at the windows. I reckon, on a Friday, he used to wish his staff a happy weekend, send them home and then waited for my call. That job set in stone for me the theory that, 'there's nowt as queer as folk'. When I told my parents about my new job my Dad said, 'What the bloody hell are you telling us for?'. I answered his question by saying, 'I thought I better had, just in case I got a request from my employers to phone you Dad', which we all had a good laugh about.

I moved into the nudey-house and asked Dennis if my Mum could come and see my new home on that Saturday afternoon. He said that was no problem at all, but to be sure to let him know what time she'd be arriving so he would get dressed for the occasion. When I was driving my Mum round to see my new place, I reassured her that Dennis wasn't going to be naked and, much to my horror, she was choked! She said that she'd only ever seen my Dad's willy, plus another three when she'd gone out with a group of ladies on a hen night and I quote, 'The first two strippers had little ones, but the last one had a whopper! His was so big that he had both of his hands on it and there was still enough left over to swing around.' I laughed so much that I almost crashed my car. My Mum was a proper lady, but every now and again she'd get very mischievous. She used to have a glint in her eye when she used to say to her sons-in-law, 'Can you trim my bush please because it's getting out of control'; she would be referring to her hydrangea bush, of course, but I'm sure she knew that her statement could of had another meaning.

Another one of her favourites was the word 'nosh'. Now, when I was a kid 'nosh' meant the contents of the old biscuit tin that she kept KitKats, Viscounts, Club biscuits and other naughty bits in. After Sunday dinner my Mum would always say to my Dad 'Henry, do you fancy a nosh?' and guaranteed he'd reply, 'I do as it happens Rose.' Before the 1990's this would have been an acceptable conversation, but then things changed when nosh became a slang word for oral sex. As my nieces got older and more streetwise, they were aware of the modern meaning of the word and used to giggle when their Nan offered their Grandad a nosh. On one of these occasions my Mum done her nut and asked what was so funny about the word nosh; I said that I'd explain it to her later, when the kids had gone home. I felt a bit embarrassed telling her, but I did. After I'd told her what its new meaning was, she said, 'Your generation are all perverts! In my day you were a slut if you let a boy put his tongue in your mouth and now you lot are kissing each other's privates.' She thought it was disgusting and said that she would continue to use the word nosh because it wasn't her problem that my generation were not only perverts, but we had perverted the English language too. I wished that I had never told her because she used that word at every given opportunity from that day on. She loved it when I took her shopping, shouting out in Sainsbury's 'I think I will buy some biscuits, just in case your father fancies a NOSH'. I thought it was so funny when she got mischievous, but some of the other shoppers thought she was a wrong-un, bless her.

In 1951, when my Mum was only twenty-one years old, she went on holiday to Austria with her friend Joan. Trust me, going abroad was very unusual back then, especially for two young women on their own. A few years after the Second World War had ended, my Mum's eldest brother, Frank, was doing his National Service in Austria, when he fell in love with and married one of the local girls, Grace. My Mum and Joan had gone to visit them, and my Mum had fallen for one of Grace's brothers. She was telling this story to her grandchildren, who were now all teenagers. She went on to explain how she and her new Austrian boyfriend had danced all night when they had first met. One of her grandchildren asked, 'Did you snog him Nan?' and she answered, 'No, I didn't snog him, but he did give me the ride of my life!'. Well, the grandchildren lost it and couldn't even speak, they were laughing so much. She left it for a while, before adding, 'The ride of my life was on the front of his pushbike, as we rode through the beautiful Austrian mountains.'

Again, did she have her mischievous head on or was her story really meant to be totally innocent? Sadly, we'll never know.

My Mum was reunited with her Austrian boyfriend many years later, when they were both in their late seventies. Sadly, it was at my Aunt Grace's funeral. When they saw each other again, both of their faces lit up like a Christmas tree and he put his hands gently on her face and said, 'Oh Rose, you have still got kissable lips'. It was a proper magical moment. My Mum went all girlie-mac-twirly but then blew it by saying, 'Thank you, I thought age had given me a mouth that looked like a cat's arse'. Everybody laughed, except for my Dad. He got all jealous and that. He had the right hump for the rest of the day. I must admit, they were flirting quite a lot and they were doing it in German, so my Dad couldn't understand what they were saying. To top it all, he kissed that 'cat's arse' mouth when they said goodbye. My Dad sulked for days, bless him.

When me and my Mum arrived at my new home Dennis was out, which I was pleased about because I got to show her all around the whole house. During her tour, she said 'Why is there a bed in the lounge?'. It was a good question, but I didn't know for sure, although I had a fairly good idea! When I informed her that it was a waterbed, she shocked me again by throwing herself backwards onto it and confessing that she'd always wanted a go on one. Her little legs shot upwards and almost hit her in the face. I joined her, and we laid there giggling like a couple of naughty kids. She said that I must never tell my Dad that she could get her legs that far up in the air, she was such a cheeky monkey at times my lovely Mum!

One night, I got back to the nudey-house very late after work. I had got a second job behind the bar in a local social club for some extra cash, just in case I fancied just one more backpacking trip! Dennis was having a party in the garden and was standing in front of a barbeque cooking burgers. He was naked except for a pinny and his bare arse was completely exposed. I must say though, well done Dennis, safety first, you don't wanna be burning ya bits!

He heard me come in and beckoned me to go join in the fun. There must have been twenty people in the garden and, apart from Dennis's pinny, not a stitch of clothing between them. I just waved and went up to bed. None of them looked like Johnny Depp so I gave it a miss. I'm sure I heard the old waterbed taking a bashing later that night; each to their own and all that. The next morning when I woke up, I got my dressing gown on and headed for the loo. To my surprise there was Dennis, right outside my door, halfway up the ladder leading to the loft. Not a stitch on as usual so all I saw was his nut-bag and his bum cheeks. 'Morning Dennis', I said, like it was just the start of another normal day, but there really was nothing 'normal' about living in that house. His office was a room directly opposite the bottom of the stairs and he would often be sat there, stark bollock naked in front of his computer, engrossed in his work. This particular morning, he heard me coming down the stairs and swivelled his chair round to talk to me; I had no idea what he was saying because I was distracted. He had his left leg bent with the foot resting on his right knee and he had failed to notice that one of his testicles was being squashed by his thigh, so much so, that it was turning a deeper shade of purple by the second. I was fascinated, I'd never seen anything like it, and I wasn't listening to a word he said because, the now almost black ball, was upstaging him totally. When he realised that I was ignoring him, he had the cheek to tell me off for being rude. I was a bit cross about his tone and asked him how he honestly expected me to have a serious conversation with him when half of his nut-bag was doing an impression of a fucking chameleon! I was still living there, very happily, when I met Brian.

It was early December 2006 and I was doing my Saturday night shift behind the bar. The night hadn't really got going so us barmaids were standing about having a chinwag. They were teasing me because I had worked there for several months and not accepted any of the date offers that had come my way. One of my work colleagues even confessed that she thought I was gay because of my short hair and lack of interest in male customers. I had grown out of my lesbian phase and was just enjoying being on my own for a change. Then Brian walked in and I thought that he was the best-looking bloke that I had ever seen in the club. He was tall, slim, bald and had very sexy and kind eyes. So, me being me, an overconfident show-off, pointed at him and said, 'Look and learn ladies, he will be mine, oh yes, he will be mine', and I went in for the kill. He didn't stand a chance really, poor Brian, he had already had a few pints in the pub down the road and he didn't know what had hit him. Within five minutes we had arranged a date for the following Sunday; I hadn't lost my touch!

I have already mentioned my number one rule to 'never sleep with a bloke if you can see the top of his head when you dance with him' but there are two more. Rule two: 'It's okay to flirt with anyone, but you can only touch if they are single'. Rule three: 'If they have got children, immediately fuck them off out of it'! Three simple little rules and I had never broken one of them, until that night. If I'm flirting with a tall, single bloke, I get this question in asap, 'Have you got any kids?' I say while my head is tilted to one side and I'm smiling as though I can't wait to hear all about their wonderful children. If the answer is 'Yes' I shut-off and walk away; only when the time is right of course, I would never be rude like. I was forty-one years old when I met Brian and had never been in a relationship with a man who had children with the exception of Nick of course, but that was different; he's the love of my life. I had successfully managed to get to this ripe old age without ever having to endure looking after my boyfriend's kids every weekend, whilst his ex-partner was off out having a great time. I truly believe that this is all due to my very clever interviewing skills. It would be different if I had kids, but I ain't, so rules is rules! With Brian I thought that, because his three children were grown up, it would be okay; I was wrong, so very, very wrong.

During mine and Brian's first date, we discovered that it had been unbelievable that we hadn't met before. Brian went to the same schools as me, but we wouldn't of met there because he was nine years older than me, but I was born and lived my first sixteen years at 85 Neverhills and he lived, from the age of two until twenty-two at 84 Neverhills, which was literally the other side of the road from me. When I was a kid I used to street-rake with Brian's younger brother Don, who was only two years my senior and who, I might add, I got arrested with once!

I was ten years old and about ten stone. I used to go through hell at school (until Sharon became my bouncer) because I was ill, fat and ginger. I can still hear the chants now, 'Big fat ginger Jew, big fat ginger Jew, you fat bastard, you fat bastard, big fat ginger

Jew' or 'fa-tty Jackie, fa-tty Jackie, fa-tty Jackie is a Jew, fa-tty Ja-ckie is a Jew', nice! I also had terrible trouble learning how to read, I was a mathematical genius, but shit at reading. When I first started senior school, I had to have special reading classes. A few minutes before the twice-weekly French lessons were about to start, in the amazing language lab that had the new invention called 'computers', this woman would walk into the classroom, clipboard in hand and shout 'Special Readers.' All of us thick kids had to then stand up and take the walk of shame to get our names ticked off her list and then follow her down the corridor. Everyone would chuck their pencils, pens and rubbers at us when we were leaving the class while shouting abuse; terrible isn't it? Imagine that happening today, no way, thankfully.

It was the year before I started senior school that Don and I broke the law. There were seven of us, all aged between eight and thirteen, playing over the garages at the back of my house. I had been told many times not to climb onto the garage roofs because I was fat and, therefore, very dangerous. I used to love the sound the roof made when I ran on it though. I just couldn't control myself and had to do it. However, I wasn't as keen on the noise the roof made seconds before it cracked and sent my fat body downwards onto a car's roof. Nor was I liking the feel, or look, of the blood escaping from the cuts on my legs and I knew my Mum wasn't going to be overly impressed with the rips in my tracksuit either. Some of the older boys (it took three of them) lifted me out of the garage and told me to get home, but not to tell my parents how I had hurt myself and just to tell them that I had fallen over. Yeah right, because they are going to fall for that when I have got bits of asbestos garage roof embedded into my flesh! I got a good hiding for that and rightly so. Later that day a policeman came to the door and said that I had to go to the station with him. Oh holy crap I was being arrested!! NOOOOOO!!! Of course, my parents knew that I wasn't actually being arrested, just being taught a lesson, but I was unaware of this plan and was petrified. I was back home within the hour, but I never went on that roof again. The reason the police had gotten involved was because when I'd gone home, the older boys had taken advantage of the new entrance to the garage and climbed down from the roof and repainted the poor garage owner's car with the various tins of paint that he had stored in there. The poor bloke would never have known who had vandalised his car, but Don, the silly bugger, had painted 'Don Wise woz ere' on the wall so we all got caught; nice one Don but serves us right.

I obviously knew Brian's parents too, via Don, and it came to light later that their Mum had lived a few doors away from my Dad's family in Dagenham, when she was a child during and after the Second World War; she even used to sit next to one of my Dad's sisters in school. Such a small world innit! Brian and I were so good together right from the word go, in every way. He was laid-back, so he calmed me down and I am neurotic, so I livened him up. We felt very relaxed in each other's company and used to say it was almost as though we were old friends, right from the start. My Mum always said that I should be with an older man. Lenny and Gavin were both six years younger than me and she used to quote the old saying, 'You will be a young man's slave or an old man's sweetheart' and she was so right in Brian's case. He was a gentle, kind, affectionate man and his lovely eyes showed just how kind he really was. I was impressed when I first went to the flat that he was renting in Basildon because it was so clean and tidy. Most of Brian's working life he'd been in the building trade but, at almost fifty, the work was getting a bit physically challenging, so he'd recently had a career change and was now working as a cashpoint machine fitter. I liked everything about my Brian. He was the one that I could see myself settling down with, for good.

Chapter 9 I married Brian, I divorced Brian, I finally got Nick

I had only been with Brian for a few weeks but had already moved out of the nudey-house and in with him. He begged me to move because he hated me living in such a strange place. He was quite old-fashioned where stuff like that was concerned. I'd been staying with Brian for a few weeks and had decided to go on a girlie night out. My friends and I were sitting in a quiet corner of the pub when I got a tap on my shoulder. I looked round and there was Nick, looking slightly pissed but as gorgeous as ever. I hadn't seen him for years and my heart flew into my mouth when he grabbed hold of me and planted a big kiss on my lips. Not a snog, no signs of public affection allowed remember, but a proper good old smacker. As we chatted, all the emotions came flooding back. I just loved him so much. There was also the added bonus that night of seeing three of his children again, who were now grown-up of course. It was equally as great to see them and I loved hearing about the happy memories they had of staying in my house with their Dad, all those years ago. What a fantastic night I had! I hardly spoke to my girlfriends, but they said they didn't mind because they enjoyed watching me 'come to life' when I was with Nick and later referred to him as 'the one that got away.'

Just before I was leaving, Nick and I went outside for a smoke together and then it all came out. He had split up with Dawn, just over two years before, and had dreamed of bumping into me from that day on. Nick was best friends with his brother-in-law, Keith, who was married to Nick's sister, Tina. Keith and Nick had been very close since the mid-nineties and even ran a small weekend gardening business together. Nick had caught Dawn out a couple of times, messing about with other blokes, but she had sworn never to do it again. He told me that three years before, he had a feeling that she was up to her old tricks again and confided in Keith, who was happy to give Nick a shoulder to cry on. Unfortunately, it transpired that she was having an affair, but this time it was with Keith! Nick was devastated but Tina took it even harder. Nick had two young kids with Dawn and Tina had two little ones with Keith, what a mess. Dawn and Keith are still together to this very day, so in their defence, they were obviously meant to be! Nick was deadly serious when he said that he missed Keith more than he did Dawn. I had to stop myself from laughing at that comment, it wasn't an appropriate time to laugh, even though it was a classic. Nick was always happier in male company, so I got what he meant. That night he told me that he was in love with me and wanted to start a relationship but, as hard as it was, I said no. Not because I was with Brian, as much as I liked him and could see a future with him, it was more to protect my heart. When I had first met Nick, he picked Helen over me, when we were sharing a bed, he dumped me for Dawn, so I was shit-scared of letting myself get into a proper relationship with him because, it was almost inevitable, that when someone better came along, he'd move on. I just couldn't risk it; Brian was a keeper, Nick wasn't. Nick was still living life like a teenager, good on him, but I was ready to slow down a bit and get on the merry-go-round with Brian. It would be a constant rollercoaster ride with Nick and I just didn't have the energy for that anymore. That night, using modern terminology, was a 'sliding doors' moment for me. When things went pear-shaped with me and Brian, I would often relive that night in the pub and wonder if I had made the correct choice. I'm a strong believer in 'what will be, will be' and 'what's meant for ya, won't go by ya' so, if I was supposed to live 'happily ever after' with Nick, the Gods would make it happen.

I was with Brian for ten years. That was good for me because my previous record had been only seven. We got married in Las Vegas by an Elvis impersonator but then had our vows blessed in a church in Basildon when we returned. There were sixteen of us at the Vegas wedding and we had a right good laugh during the five days that we were there. Although Brian was my third husband, the wedding blessing was really like my fourth wedding, so I kept it small and only had the nine bridesmaids!! They all looked gorgeous. The eldest Mollie, aged fourteen, (the daughter of my friend that I went on holiday with to Faliraki, when I met husband number two) looked amazing in her long navy dress and the other eight, all aged seven and under, wore super-cute little white Cinderella dresses. I also wore a navy dress, to match Mollie, but I had a bride's bouquet and all that. Harry and Marie kindly transformed their car into a wedding car and drove Mollie and I to the church, and later, Brian and I from the church to the reception, love them for doing that and for taking the most wonderful photographs of the day and creating an album that had our Vegas photos and our blessing photos in, it was great. My Dad got taken ill on the day of the blessing, which unfortunately was a regular occurrence at that time, so I asked my ex-brother-in-law Burt, to give me away. Burt has always been like the big brother I always wanted. I was only twelve when Chrissie met Burt and I have loved him from that day on. I was hoping that by Burt giving me away this time, my luck might change! Perhaps my divorces were my Dad's fault, he may have been a jinx!

Brian and I only ever had one problem, and I mean just the one, we were so happy and contented with each other apart from when his family were involved. We had led such different lives, until we met. He had married his childhood sweetheart; they'd had three children together and then divorced and I'd never had kids but had travelled a lot instead to make up for it. We liked such different things too, but we worked all of our differences out quite easily. Holidays, for example. He didn't want crazy holidays, he liked all-inclusive, relaxing, luxury breaks, which we had once or twice a year. We went to some beautiful places, our favourite being Dubai and our least favourite, Margarita. Oh my Christ, the resort we stayed in was awful. It was so dirty, there were flies and wasps everywhere and the food was rank. The island itself was beautiful, but Brian didn't get to see much of it. I went on all the trips on my own, because he got salmonella, due to the dodgy food, on our first day there; the poor bastard was ill for the entire two weeks. He couldn't even stand up to do a wee because, if he did, his bowels would open, and he'd do a bum-wee at the same time. He lost two stone while we were there. At one point I thought he was gonna die. Saying that, I almost killed him one day of that holiday. We were laying round the pool, me sipping cocktails and him water, when he thought it'd be funny to chuck his pint of 'iced' water onto my belly. Not a good idea because my guts weren't too good either. The shock of the cold on my hot stomach made my bowels open quite dramatically! The pool area was packed, and I had a bikini on so to say it was embarrassing would be an understatement. I've never been so pleased to get home as after that holiday. As much as I enjoyed the so called 'posh' holidays, I still felt the need to properly explore the many other parts of the world that I was yet to experience.

To satisfy my adventurous side, my dear friend William took over. He is no longer with us I'm sorry to say, he took his own life two years ago after receiving very unjustified hate mail from an ex-lover of his. I was devastated because life without him will never be the same again, he is sadly missed. William and I had been good friends ever since he came to work at my Top Man store in Lakeside. That was twenty-four years ago when he was only seventeen and me thirty. He was gay and thirteen years younger than me, so our friendship was an unlikely one, but I saw him more regularly than I did any of my other friends; he was incredibly needy and slightly narcissistic but I never minded because he amused me lots. We had been to so many places together that I could quite easily write an entire book, solely about our holidays and his odd ways. It was only four years ago that we hired a brand-new convertible Mustang and drove through six American states, all in a three-week period. During that adventure, he talked me into doing a tandem skydive over Salt Lake City! We'd been to see Niagara Falls, drove over a thousand miles from Vancouver to Calgary in Canada, done New York and too many other places to mention. If I had gone with Nick in my 'sliding doors' moment and not Brian, William and I would never of experienced half of the things that we had. Brian was mega-understanding about my lust to travel but Nick, not so much so.

I often went away for weekends with my Mum and sister too and Brian never minded at all. I think he used to enjoy the peace and quiet, truth be told. We went to Devon mainly, to see some of my Mum's family; three of her brothers had moved there when I was little. We used to stay in cheap bed and breakfast places and have a right good laugh. When she was in her eighties, the three of us went to a family wedding in Omagh, Northern Ireland. It was in December and the temperature plummeted to minus eighteen! Of course, the thick snow made the wedding photos amazingly beautiful, but driving was a nightmare, as was going outside for us dirty smokers to have a fag. Nobody managed to smoke more than half a fag at a time (because you could feel your lungs icing up) except for my Mum. She was hardcore. Every time she went out, she'd smoke a whole fag, and they were 'luxury length' ones. She used to say, 'I do enjoy a luxury length', again, with that cheeky glint in her eye. During the evening she got up 'again' to have a smoke and I begged her not to go outside because it was absolutely freezing. She'd been gone a while, so I went to look for her. She wasn't outside, oh no, she was in our posh hotel room, hanging out of the window, puffing away. Naughty, but bloody funny.

Mine and Brian's 'only' problem was that he'd split-up with his wife, Lyn, when their children were still quite young, and he adopted the 'weekend Dad' mentality from that day on. Brian and Lyn had been divorced for twelve years when I met him, but his daughters, not his son, treated me as though I was the wicked bitch that had taken their Daddy away from their Mummy! I don't know why; I used to have sleepless nights trying to analyse it, but I just didn't understand. Perhaps I tried too hard from the day that I met them, but in my defence, I had never had a boyfriend with kids before and I didn't know how to play that game. It wasn't only the daughters that I had aggro from, it was

Lyn and her best friend and the sister-in-law, who was married to my old mucker Don. I let all of them treat me like absolute shit for ten whole years. It's just so not like me. I am normally very good at sticking up for myself but whenever they were bullying me, I never once retaliated because I didn't want to upset Brian or Don, so I took it on the chin. I'm not being dramatic using the word 'bullying'. There is honestly no other word to describe how they treated me. We didn't see them that often which is why I allowed it to go on for so long, I think. Brian thought that his kids could do no wrong; their shit didn't stink! If, after a day in hell with them, I would ask Brian if he thought their behaviour towards me was acceptable, he would go on the turn and start screaming at me and turning it around like it was my fault. So, I gave up trying to make him see them for what they were.

What happened when my Mum died should have been the end of the marriage, but I even forgave him for that. My Dad had told us all, every Christmas Day for the past seventeen years, that this would be his last Christmas and used to make us all raise our glasses, to him! My Mum, however, was eighty-three years old and had only been in hospital once in her entire lifetime and that was to give birth to Chrissie in 1960. She walked out of that hospital with her new-born baby in her arms and said to my Dad, 'I hated it in hospital, and I am never going to one again' and true to her word, she didn't!

Once a year, always just after Christmas, she would get a bout of bronchitis, stop smoking, take antibiotics, get over it, job done. She was so lucky with her health and only got her yearly illness because she was a smoker. It was naughty really, but we were always so pleased when she went back on the fags, after she'd been ill, because we knew that meant that she was feeling better. The only time she had to visit the hospital was to have an X-ray, when she was seventy-nine, because she was getting into the back of a taxi and the driver shot away before she'd got all the way in. The wheel arch caught her leg, she was catapulted into the air and landed on the tarmac. My parents were on their way to their youngest granddaughter's eighteenth birthday party and she wouldn't have missed that for the world, so she got up and insisted on getting into the taxi and off they went. When she arrived, we were all mortified; her knees were bleeding, she had gravel in her hair and blood on her shoulder. She insisted that she felt fine, so we cleaned her up and she spent the next six hours drinking wine, eating vol au vents, dancing and, get this, 'pole dancing'. The venue had a huge pole in the middle of the dance floor (one would assume that they had strippers there at times) and she loved it. The next day, her shoulder looked very bruised and she had to admit, was hurting but she refused to go to the hospital. It wasn't until the Tuesday, three days later, that she let me take her. The hospital informed us that she had a broken collarbone and told her off for not seeing them sooner. She never made a fuss and just carried on as normal. A year later we celebrated her eightieth at the same place. We had a great time, but she was a bit upset that the pole had been removed!

Brian and I were going to London one Saturday with some friends, but we popped in for a cuppa with my parents before we went. They were both fine. I used to see my Mum and Dad almost every day; not because I felt that I had to, but because I wanted to. My Mum was my best friend and my Dad was always a good laugh and very entertaining so who wouldn't want to visit them? I got a phone call that night, whilst travelling back from London, from Malcolm, saying that my Mum had collapsed on the bedroom floor and an ambulance was on the way. They were putting her lifeless body onto a stretcher when I arrived. She was just about hanging on in there, but I knew that her soul had already gone home. The hospital staff were brilliant. They tried everything to make her well again and said they had to give her the best chance possible, due to the fact that she had only been in hospital once before. They were truly gobsmacked by that fact, especially because she'd been a smoker for almost seventy years. The doctors kept her heart and lungs going, with help from various equipment, for a few days but her little body gave in and she died in my arms on her hospital bed, having never fully regained consciousness since she fell onto the bedroom floor on the Saturday night. It was a terrible shock for everyone that loved her because she hadn't been ill, but I will be forever grateful that when her number had come up, she had just collapsed with no suffering, no pain, no having to endure messing herself or forgetting her loved one's names. It was just 'oh well, that's me lot now, bye-bye'.

Chrissie and I did the necessary pre-funeral business over the next few days. Our Dad had been housebound for years, but although we consulted him on everything, we did it all and had never been so close as we were that week and our strong sisterly love has continued ever since. Our Mum died on the Tuesday night, we did the legal stuff on the Wednesday and Thursday so, by Thursday night there was nothing left to do, apart from wait for the day of the funeral. It was on that Thursday night that Brian asked me to write down the details of the funeral because he wanted to tell his kids. I couldn't understand because they wouldn't have been attending the funeral, they hardly knew my Mum and they'd made no effort to talk to her when their paths had crossed in the past. She had said many times, 'Brian's kids make me feel invisible.' To be honest, it was nothing personal towards my Mum because if ever we mixed the families, 'all' my lot were invisible to his kids, and to him! He was a brilliant uncle to my nieces, and he loved them dearly, as they did him, however, if his family were there, he honestly, I swear, never even looked at any of my lot and was just all over his family like a rash. This used to really upset my girls and parents, but Brian was normally so lovely when they weren't around, that they let it go. There were a few times that I had to stop my Mum and nieces from giving his kids a gob full however, because they hated seeing me treated so horrifically badly!

I asked Brian if his kids had said that they wanted to attend the funeral and he said that they hadn't yet, but he was sure they would. I was very calm because I'd been mentally raped over the previous few days, obviously, my Mum had dropped dead with no warning and her little body was laying on a slab somewhere as we spoke so I had no mental energy left for an argument. I simply asked if he would mind, if they did ask, to tell them not to attend because he would be needed to be 'Uncle Brian' that day and be there to support the nieces and perhaps even me, which would be nice! That was it, he went crazy and said that I had no right to tell his kids what to do or not do because I was nothing to them and he ended the 'screaming in my face session' by calling me a 'cunt'. He had never called me that before, in fact nobody ever had and the timing for that little word being shouted into my face was despicable! My Mum's funeral was sixteen days later, and he hadn't said a single word to me, or touched or cuddled me, until six days before the cremation took place. His kids didn't even want to come; I knew they wouldn't. We gave my Mum the best send-off ever; I'm sure she would have been proud of us.

Life carried on, but it was never the same again. How could it be when the most amazing wife, Mum, Nan and Great-Nan (Little Nanny) had been taken away from us? My last thought at night and my first thought in the morning, wasn't about my Mum like you would imagine, it was that evening when Brian had called me a cunt. This went on for over a year, until my Dad died. His death was so much more dramatic, just the way he would have wanted. He had LBS until his dying breath, love him.

It's mad because we were all shocked when he died, even though he'd been practising dying for seventeen long years. Everyone assumed that he'd not last long after my Mum died, but that was so not the case. When I used to tell people that my parents hadn't liked each other for many years, they'd disagree and say that there was still a lot of love there and that would become apparent when one of them goes, but I knew I was right. A few weeks before my Mum had died, I went to see them both, and the atmosphere was even worse than normal; they had obviously had another argument. When I asked what was wrong, my Dad informed me that my Mum had hit him. Apparently, the first punch (oh yeah, there was more than one, she'd proper battered him) caught him right on the chin, the second was to his arm but he'd managed to dodge the third. I asked her why she'd felt the need to hit my Dad and she said, 'He drives me bleedin' mad, he's got old before his time (he was eighty-two) and he's arsehole lucky that he hasn't got the letter opener hanging out the side of his neck'. Harsh, but I couldn't help but chuckle to myself. Days before this incident, I arrived at their flat just as my Dad was being stretchered into an ambulance. He had a severe chest infection and could hardly breathe. I told my Mum to get in with him and I'd follow in my car and meet them there. She lit up a fag and looked at me as though I had gone mad and said, 'Don't be ridiculous, I can't smoke in an ambulance', and proceeded to get into my car. I pointed out that she couldn't smoke in the car either, so she reluctantly got out, dabbed her fag out, put it back into the box and got into the ambulance with her angry face on. True love that is.

When my Mum was stretchered into an ambulance, days before she died, I told my Dad that I'd take him and his wheelchair to the hospital. He said, 'Turn it in Jackie, I ain't going out there, it's bleedin' freezing', and then told me not to bring her back home if she was in a state because he didn't want to be sitting next to her if she was gonna be brain-damaged and shitting herself every five minutes. Alrighty then, understood.

Chrissie phoned him every day from the hospital to ask if he wanted to come to see our Mum, perhaps to say goodbye, but every time he said, 'What's the bloody point in that, I've been with the woman for sixty years, don't you think we've said everything we need to say to each other by now'? The night she died it was late and he'd already told us not to phone him later than 10pm or earlier than 9am because he needed his kip, so we didn't go around to tell him until the following morning - after nine of course. He was a selfish git, so he wasn't trying to hide his feelings to make us feel better, he was genuinely okay. He was upset that he couldn't go to the funeral though, but we agreed with his decision. It was such a bitterly cold and windy day that he said, 'If I go out in this weather to the crematorium, you'll be leaving me up there'. He had a point. However, there was a wonderful moment during all this. We don't really do flowers at funerals, we prefer it if people make a donation to charity, but he insisted on having flowers from him. When I gave him the card that was going on his flowers, he simply wrote 'My Wife, My Life'. Amazing.

The next six months were unbelievable. He started to eat well, which was unheard of, and he put on loads of weight. He said, 'It's so nice not having to eat the terrible grub ya mother used to cook'. He was loving the microwave meals he'd started to have; he couldn't get enough of them. The old bastard also used to say, quite often, 'It's great, I don't have to watch all the old shit on telly that she liked anymore', he was well happy with his new life! The most shocking thing was, for the first time in years, he started to go out on his electric scooter again. Almost every lunchtime he used to go to the pub, have a couple of pints and then pop in the betting shop before going home. Unfortunately, after six months of enjoying his life as a widower, his health started to go downhill, and he eventually died fourteen months after my Mum.

The night he died, Brian actually said to me, 'I fucked up a bit (A FUCKING BIT!!!) when your Mum died, but I will make it up to you now.' I wanted to say 'Make up for it? Oh fuck off Brian, I've got more important things to think about at the moment, like grieving for my Dad for one, you idiot' but I bit my tongue.

A few months after my Dad had died, Brian decided that sixteen of us were going on holiday to Portugal, his treat, for his forthcoming sixtieth birthday. The guest list was Brian, me, his three kids, their partners and the eight grandchildren. 'This should be interesting' I thought 'A whole week of being treated like 'that word' that he had called me when my Mum died'; I could hardly wait. How wrong could I have been because it turned out to be one of the best holidays that I've ever had, and his daughters finally noticed how truly wonderful and excellent I was! The grandchildren had all realised my fantastic-ness right from birth, as had Brian's son since the first day I met him, but the others also opened their eyes on that holiday and saw it too. We all, after ten years, bonded. I was so happy because nothing would ever break me and Brian up now and this really was the beginning of a perfect marriage. I was willing to let go of all the shit in the past and just look forward. It was probably the happiest and most contented that I had ever been. Life was going to be stress-free and chilled from now on.

The next few months were so nice; his daughters even started to phone me and send me text messages. Even the ex-wife and her sidekick started to include me in conversations, instead of turning their backs on me to cut me out like normal. Well, it was nice while it lasted, but of course all good things must come to an end. I was hoping it would last for more than three fucking months though! I had been the shit on their shoes for ten years, then up on a pedestal for three months when Brian's youngest daughter kicked the pedestal away and I came crashing down to the floor again! Well done you horrible shit-bags, you pulled a blinder and finally managed to get me out of Brian's life; it took them ten years though! I had turned up thirty minutes late to a family barbeque, get this, because I was visiting Brian's pregnant daughter-in-law who was in hospital and had phoned me and begged me to go see her. I wasn't visiting one of my family, it was one of his! Brian's youngest daughter, the hostess of the barbeque, didn't like the fact that I'd turned up late and she didn't care what the reason was. There were about twenty people at the do, so I doubt if anyone had even really noticed that I wasn't there. It wasn't a surprise party so surely getting there, bang-on time wasn't that important, but she was playing the 'youngest child, little princess' card, told her Dad that my lateness had really upset her and managed to convince him that I was out of order. He was seriously angry with me and when we got back home, he not only screamed, and I'm talking evil, nasty, in my face screaming, but he also pushed me up against the wall. I swear that he would have punched my face in if I hadn't of started crying and saying 'sorry', over and over again. I'd had a taste of domestic abuse years before and was sure as shit not going down that road again, so the next day I said just three little words to him, here we go yet again 'Unacceptable, fuck off'. We were divorced within eight weeks because, thankfully, he signed the paperwork to admit that his behaviour had been unreasonable. I have never seen or heard from Brian, or any of his family, ever since. Every single day I miss being 'Nanny Jackie' and I will love the beautiful grandchildren, him, his son and son in laws, very much for the rest of my life, but the rest of them I will never miss for a single second, that's for sure.

I will admit that I was in a mess when Brian left because 'we'
didn't want to break up, 'they' wanted us to and the injustice of
the situation was making me ill. My fighting weight has been ten
stone for years. I feel good at that weight, unlike in my younger
days when my weight would be 'up and down like a whore's
drawers' as my Mum used to say. Within six weeks I had gone
down to eight stone, not good. I looked so old and haggard and
had sores on my hip bones because there was just no meat on me.
I was eating, but my metabolism had gone as crazy as had I. I've
always battled with my weight and have been going to 'fat clubs'
most of my adult life, but I tell you now, as hard as it is to lose
weight, it's so much harder to put it on. My Scarlet is built like
my Mum; she's a tiny little thing and is constantly trying to
chub-up. She gets so angry when people comment on her size by
saying things like, 'Get some meat on your bones, you're too
skinny.' As she rightly points out, in our society its acceptable to
call somebody 'skinny' or 'thin' but if she was to say to an
overweight person 'You are well fat, you should get yourself on

a diet and lose that excess blubber' they would be insulted and she would get a mouthful of abuse, or worse, they could sit on her and that would be the last we ever saw of Scarlet, she'd spend the rest of her days wedged between some fatties bum cheeks!

My Mum was fifteen years old when the Second World War ended so had experienced living on rations. This had made her a 'fattist' and she thought that being fat meant that you were simply greedy. If I put on as much as a pound in weight, I'm telling ya, she would notice. When I first took husband number two to my parent's house for a Sunday afternoon 'nosh', she proper embarrassed me. I was about nine and a half stone at the time and had only met Lenny in Faliraki a few weeks before, so we were in the honeymoon period, not even on farting terms. The four of us were in the lounge, chatting away, when I leant forward to get my second item out of the nosh tin, she said 'Should you be having another one?'. Lenny looked confused and replied to my Mum's comment by saying 'But Jackie is very slim.' I started to get tense because I knew what was coming. 'Oh yes' she said, 'at the moment, but you don't know how far her skin can stretch.' Oh well, he had to find out at some point that I was a fat bird trapped inside a skinny bird's body.

I was dreading my first Christmas without Brian and the grandchildren. He'd left in the September, so I had three months to get mentally stronger to get through the festive period. It's always an emotional time for me, especially since my parents died.

It wasn't happening so I went to my retreat which is Harry and Marie's welcoming and fun home in Yorkshire. I love going up there to spend time with my wonderful friends. The three of us always walk for miles, to enable us to experience as much of the beautiful scenery as possible, it's very therapeutic. My life is always busy, a bit too much so to be honest. I always work full-time and am a lucky girl because I have an abundance of people in my life that love me dearly and want to spend time with me. The only problem is, there are so many of them. Lots of people cross our paths in our lifetimes and, as much as we would like them to, they can't 'all' stay on it forever, it is only a path after all, not a four-lane motorway! This is why, sometimes I have to, as I call it, 'delete' people. I really, really, hate doing it, but if I don't, I wouldn't have the time to work or sleep, there are only so many hours in a day. Someone said to me once, that my problem is that I make everyone feel like they are my best friend. I know what she means, but I genuinely love 'all' my friends and work colleagues and feel guilty, every day of my life, because I am not spending enough time with them. I hate mobile phones because it is too easy to get hold of me. I get so many text messages from my loved ones asking when I can go visit them. I'm permanently stressed, and guilt-ridden; it ain't good. When I'm not in a relationship, things get a bit easier because I only have to worry about finding the time to see my lot. My family are my world and the ones that I like to spend my free time with, but

I try to find time to see my wonderful friends too. After working a five-day week, followed by a day of life-maintenance shit, I've only got Sundays and it's just impossible to do twenty visits in one day. There are the evenings after work of course, so I do get to socialise a bit then, but I'm getting older and need my beauty sleep so I can't spend every school night out on a jolly. I think that is why I used to travel a lot. When I felt as though there were too many plugs in my socket and that I was about to fuse, I'd bugger off for a while to recharge. When my head is in a happy place I don't stress about stuff as much, but after losing Brian it was all getting to me. However, I felt much better, as always, after my Yorkshire break.

A week before Christmas, Chrissie invited all the family to hers for a get- together, as she does quite often; she and Malcolm are amazing hosts and love having everyone round. It was an evening do so there was going to be booze involved, better still. I hadn't touched alcohol since Brian had left because I'd been on the old happy pills for the first time in my life, and the two don't mix well. I was feeling well enough after seeing Harry and Marie, to be pill-free and ready to have a pre-Christmas piss-up! Chrissie had asked me to bring some of my many home movies along. I was the only one to have had a video camera in the family years ago. You can afford expensive items like that when you don't have kids! My videos, now on DVD, go back to when Scarlet was about two years old. We all enjoy sitting around the TV and laughing at how we all looked in the 1980's and 90's. A few tears are normally shed too, when we see the people on the screen that are no longer with us, either due to death or divorce!

I was having a great time and loving spending time with my nieces; they are all so very different, but all equally as special and great to be around. Scarlet is so much like her Dad, Burt. Very rarely does she stress about anything, she takes life one step at a time and often says to me, normally when I'm having one of my famous rants, 'It is what it is' although I know that she does think deeply about things, but removes the stress element from her mind and just gets on with it. When she was a little girl, she loved Michael Jackson, so I took her to Wembley Stadium to see him. That was the only time that I've seen her cry with joy. When he first appeared on the stage, she burst into tears and said, 'It's like a dream come true'. I took her to a Donny Osmond concert years later when she was in her early twenties. Her reaction wasn't quite the same. As we walked into the arena, she could see that she was the youngest one in there. It was full of middle-aged women and she said, 'Oh God, I can smell nothing but hormone patches and Tena Ladies'. She cried when my Donny walked onto the stage too, but they were tears of laughter I suspect! She's excellent and has been with her Doug for years now. They have a beautiful little doggie called Betsie and the three of them live very happily together in their lovely flat. I call her the 'eldest and wisest' niece. Then there's my Rosie who has been with her husband, Sid, since she was sixteen and they are still so totally devoted to each other. They now have two kids,

Ruby and Seany. Their first child, Darren, sadly died at only a week old, but he is talked about and missed, often; he's gone, but certainly not forgotten. Ruby and Seany know that they have a big brother in the spirit world and their parents take them to visit their big brother's grave from time to time. I call Rosie 'weird niece' because she is! She loves nothing more than talking about spiritualism and paganism. She has a fascination regarding where we go when we fall off our perches. This is my fault really because, until life got too busy, I was also right into all that witchy stuff. When she was a kid she was forever coming out with inappropriate things, in total innocence I must add. When she was about six, we were all playing Eye Spy. The letter was 'D' and she started jumping with joy and shouted out 'Dickhead'. Bless her, she got all embarrassed when she was told that it was a rude word. She is the most caring and thoughtful of my nieces and a loving wife and Mum. Next is Georgia, but I call her 'chav-niece' because she has got a bit of the 'chavs' about her. A lady that I used to work with thought that was her actual name.

She said that she wasn't keen on unusual names but did like my niece's name 'Chavniece', lol. She was such a funny child and the way her mind worked never ceased to amaze me. We were in a graveyard, trying to find her great-grandmother's grave, when she was only about ten. We were walking up and down the rows for ages when she went on the turn and shouted, 'This is ridiculous, why don't they bury people in alphabetical order?'. Priceless. Georgia has also been with her childhood sweetheart, our Vinnie, for many years and they are Mummy and Daddy to Franchesca and Heidi. I am very close to Georgia and she is the most like me out of the four girls. We talk almost every day and she has done a bloody good job at taking over from my Mum, especially on the friendship front. She has got a wicked sense of humour, is quick-witted, very confident, can be quite loud and has a heart of gold. Last, but by no means least, we have Gracie 'baby niece' (she is actually twenty-seven now, so perhaps I should rename her) who has just had her first baby with a little help from her gorgeous partner, my sexy Jimmy, who tends to bring out the pervy Auntie Jackie in me, as does Georgia's Vinnie. I was so delighted when Gracie and Jimmy named their baby 'Henry' after my little Dad; he would have been chuffed. Gracie is a Daddy's girl and has lots of his traits too, all the good ones of course. She has done very well career-wise and is even more laid-back than Scarlet and quite shy. As a child she was super-clumsy and, like Rosie, used to come out with some corkers. As stated previously, someone would always propose a toast to Aunt Bessie on Christmas Day. When Gracie was about ten, she asked, 'I've wanted to know for years now, who actually is Aunt Bessie?'. Bless her scatty little head! Gracie is her happiest when she is with her Jimmy, and now her Henry too of course.

It was during the pre-Christmas piss-up, whilst watching my old videos, that Georgia asked who the bloke was that seemed to be in lots of the footage; I told her it was Nick. Scarlet and Rosie remembered him because he would always bring his eldest two children, Nick and Chloe, to all their birthday parties when they were little, but Georgia and Gracie were too young to remember. Georgia being Georgia, insisted that I told her all about him and she managed to get the entire 'Jackie and Nick' love story out of me. She always has to know the ins and out of a duck's arse that girl. She informed me that the whole family were getting bored of seeing me all thin and depressed and said, 'You need to get yourself another man to cheer you up. What about that Nick?'. I was a bit tipsy, so agreed to let her try to find Nick on Facebook.

I hate all that social media bollocks, it's killing the art of conversation and nothing seems to be private anymore; not even what people are having for their tea. 'I've got spag bol tonight, yum, yum' and they prove it by posting a picture of their dinner! Oh fuck off, I don't give a shit what you're eating but thanks for taking a picture of a spaghetti bolognese because I have never seen one before!! Why don't these people try doing something useful like perhaps phoning a loved one for a chat, you know, actually using words and that. Tell them you were thinking of them and that you love them, there's an idea for ya, try it, you might enjoy it! My favourite is when I go out for a meal, I bet there will be half a dozen families, dining out, not saying a single word to each other. The Mum, Dad and the kids all playing with their electronic devices and couples, again, totally ignoring each other and just looking at their phone. What's the fucking point of going out? Surely, they could have been antisocial zombies at home, and it would have been cheaper! Go get a fucking life you freaks! Soz, I've finished now. However, Facebook can be handy when you manage to track down the love of your life. Everybody knows that 'drunk texting' is never a good idea but all logic goes out the window in these circumstances, plus he looked so sexy in his profile picture; just like I remembered him, if not better. Georgia sent a Facebook message to him, saying that we were having a family night, he was in lots of the videos and her Auntie Jackie would love to hear from him and left my mobile number.

It seemed like a great idea at the time, but the next morning I wasn't sure it had been a good move.

I didn't hear from him for a good few days, but Georgia said that was because he hadn't checked his Facebook. Finally, he did and texted me straight away; my belly went all funny, I was thrilled. Even if he was in a relationship, I was hoping that we could still have a catch-up because I often wondered how he was doing and still missed him and cared about him very much. We sent loads of text messages back and forth which I would never normally do, I hate texting, I prefer a chat, but I had a chest and throat infection and sounded like Frank Bruno! He said, in one of the messages, that I always did sound like Frank, so what was new? We arranged to meet in a nearby pub on the evening of the twenty-third of December. It was a Friday and was going to be my last day at work before the Christmas nine-day break. I made it crystal clear in my messages that I was in-between husbands but, the clever sod made no reference to his relationship status;

he knew what he was doing, the bugger. I finished my last day at work and got home by 3pm. I shaved my legs, pits and bikini line, just in case, put a nice dress on, done my hair and waited for his text to say that he had finished work and was on his way to the pub. After two hours of waiting and two glasses of red wine later, I decided to go get my stockings on, again, just in case. Another hour passed, so, very unusual for me, I put some make-up on. Then I was getting a bit nervous, so I texted him. He said he would be there in an hour. I wasn't in the mood for the pub really and I knew it would be rammed, so I asked if he would mind coming straight to my flat instead. I had a lasagne in the freezer so I could chuck that in the oven if he fancied a nosh!....see what I did there? When he knocked on my door my legs almost gave way, it was like that 'Blind Date' programme. My hands were shaking as I went to open the door, I was too frightened to open it, but I did and there he was, my gorgeous Nick. He was a bit thin, like my good self, but looking as handsome as ever and his arms were full of Christmas presents. Oh fuck, I hadn't thought of doing that, embarrassing!! He came strutting in, plonked the presents onto the dining room table and gave me a big cuddle. I melted, it felt absolutely fan-fucking-tastic to be back in his arms and I was praying, that he was single. I opened my presents, all of which I loved by the way, he obviously still knew me very well and then I started trying to find out if he was single. He was, so I showed him my stockings and started flirting uncontrollably and a good time was then had by all!!! We didn't only have sexy-time, but a good old laugh too and did lots of catching up. We had one sad moment when he told me that he had heard that my Dad had died and asked how my Mum was doing. He obviously hadn't been informed that my Mum had actually died before him. It was horrible, I didn't know how to tell him because he truly loved my parents and he already had tears in his eyes about my Dad's death. I opted for the short and sweet option and answered him by saying, 'She's dead.' Perhaps if I'd sugar-coated it a bit he may not have been quite so upset, but as I always say, 'Regret is a wasted emotion!'. He stayed the night and the next morning took me to see his house.

When he had finally moved out of my house, in the early 1990's, he had moved into digs next door to his new girlfriend, Dawn, and her family. The council refused to give him accommodation even though he had his four kids every weekend, so he was forced to buy a house; that was twenty-four-years before, and he still lived in it. He warned me that it wasn't in the best state of repair, but I was still a bit shocked when I saw it. A few weeks later my Georgia went to see it. She told Nick that she thought it looked like a crack den. She said it right to his face like, don't hold back Georgia, say it as it is, why don't ya! She does make me proud that girl. I was more diplomatic than her on my first visit because I could see the potential it had. It was a nice big three bedroom place but needed some TLC. He seemed to have started doing things in every room, but never actually finished the job. He was still working ridiculously long hours and just never had time to sort the house out. It was clean, but in a bit of a state. Nick has always loved a big, real Christmas tree and there was one in his lounge, but it was bare.

Again, he had got the tree but not finished it. He had bags of decorations and lights to decorate it with on the floor next to it, so I suggested that we decorated it together. It was Christmas Eve and there I was in my Nick's house, making a Christmas tree come to life. What a wonderful way to be ending a fucking awful year. It was a movie moment. We were laughing and mock arguing as we made the tree look amazing. We obviously had a reminisce about the Mad Mindy Christmas tree saga too! He had plans to go out with his mates that night and was umming and ahhing about still going because we were having a great time, but I insisted that he went. So, we said our goodbyes and planned to get together again in a few days.

I had been dreading waking up alone on Christmas morning but, as it turned out, I had no need to. I went to bed that night, but not at all sad. I went off to sleep whilst doing a post-mortem, in my head, of the last twenty-four hours that I had just spent with Nick and was feeling all toasty inside, lovely. At three o'clock in the morning there was a knock on the door and there was Nick. Now normally, if anyone ever wakes me up, I am a nasty piece of work, unless it's an emergency of course, but I was so happy to see him. He had walked in the freezing cold, over two miles from the club he had been to, just to say, 'Merry Christmas my darling.' We went to sleep but I had to wake him up a few hours later because I was due to go to Chrissie and Malcolm's for the day and was staying at their place for the night too. Nick was going to spend the day alone. I did ask if he wanted to join us, Chrissie and Malcolm would have loved that, but he was feeling a bit rough and wanted to go home. For many years he had spent Christmas Day alone and then, on Boxing Day, all six of his kids, their partners and the grandchildren would go visit him and end up having an all-night party. I had a great time at Chrissie's; all the kids and her grandchildren were there, it was lovely. All the usual activities; opening gifts, playing games and ending the festivities with a good old singsong and a boogie.

On Boxing Day I was going out for dinner with friends but had said that I may pop into Nick's to see him and his kids on the way home. I phoned him as I left the restaurant and his party was in full swing. They were all shouting out nice things to me on the phone and saying they were so happy I was with their Dad and how they were dying to see me again. I was stone-cold sober because I was driving and lost my bottle. Obviously, Nick's kids were nothing like Brian's daughters, but I was so frightened in case one of them said the slightest derogatory remark to me, I know that I would have lost it.

All the horrible memories came flooding back of how Brian's family would barely say hello to me and then make sure the conversations had nothing to do with me. How, on the rare occasion that I would try to join in, they would look at me, stony-faced, without saying a word, raise their eyebrows, look at each other, leave a pause and then say 'Anyway, as I was saying' and carry on the conversation. One of the nastiest things they ever did to me was, ironically, on a Boxing Day get-together. Brian's ex-wife Lyn had invited the whole family, and us, to her house. The evening started with a buffet in her kitchen where she told several stories about the Christmases that she, Brian and the children had spent together before they had parted. One of the stories, which she told while laughing her head off, was about how she had got so drunk one Christmas Day that when they went to bed and started 'making love' that she had been sick! Nice! Classy! That was way too much information for my liking. I tell cheeky stories at times, but I liken them to the humour of the 'Carry On' films. Hers were way too detailed and graphic. I tried so hard during that meal to 'get in' but was shut down time after time. If they were all laughing about something that had been said and I then chucked a comment in, honest to God, it would go quiet, the eyebrows would go up again, they took a sip of their drink and continued, never even making eye contact with me. I hated it when they were all standing in a circle and I would try to join them. They would literally turn their backs to me, un-fucking-believable!! This was how it always was, well, until the holiday in Portugal. Brian's two sons-in-law were wonderful lads and used to feel my pain and look at me with their heads on the side. They'd even give me the occasional affectionate squeeze of a bingo wing if they could manage it without their partners seeing. The girls would have gone mad at their boyfriends if they'd caught them being nice to me! Photographs are always taken at family get-togethers of course and I always hated that bit because they would, every single time, ask me to take the pictures to make sure that I wasn't in any of them. Several times they actually physically, albeit gently, pushed me away from their Dad to enable them to get a picture without me in it. Both of their Facebook pages had so many pictures on, hundreds in fact, and I wasn't in one of them; their Mum's partner was, but never me. When Brian and I had our wedding blessing lots of pictures were taken, so I looked at their Facebook pages and there were lots of them on there. Guess how many I was in? Yeah, now you're getting it, 'None'! That must have taken some doing really because I was the bride! It must have been very time-consuming, cropping so many photos to get shot of me!

After we had eaten Lyn's Boxing Day evening dinner, we were invited to go into the lounge to play a game. She had a huge corner sofa, so everyone fitted on except for one; that'll be me on the floor then. The game was 'Family Fortunes' but oh no, there were thirteen people in the room so it would have to be six on each team; someone wouldn't be able to play. Yes, that'll be me again then. Brian didn't say a word, but the youngest daughter's partner did, bless him, but not about me being excluded from the sofa or the game but, he stood up and said, 'For fuck's sake Jackie, please stand up, but do it slowly.' I was leant against a radiator cover that hadn't been fixed to the wall properly and this lad had clocked that the ex-wife, the sidekick and the daughters had been giggling and waiting for me to fidget a bit which would of made the big vase that was on top of the radiator cover, come crashing down onto my head. That lovely lad saved me a visit to the Accident and Emergency department of Basildon Hospital. It would have cut my head open if he hadn't of warned me. It's unbelievable really when I look back, and I was looking back a lot, on this Boxing Day, hence why I didn't risk going to see Nick and his lot; just in case. Brian's family had broken me and my faith in human nature.

My fears were ridiculous really because the following month Nick had a birthday party in his house. I went and was totally overwhelmed by how lovely they all were to me. It was the first time I had met his youngest two, Abigail and Ellie that he'd had with Dawn, and I instantly loved them as much as I already loved the eldest four. Ellie, the youngest, started crying late that night. When I gave her a cuddle and asked why she was upset, she said, 'These are happy tears because I have never seen Dad so happy before'. Ellie was very young when Nick and Dawn had separated and for the past twelve years Nick had been single, so this was the first time she'd seen her Dad with a girlfriend. Bless her for loving her Dad so much that his happiness had reduced her to tears. They all adore their father, and rightly so, he would do anything for his children, and I think he's a great Dad.

Chapter 10 The future

Mine and Nick's relationship took off as though we'd never been apart. It was perfect. We were both so happy, content and used to laugh every day about the past and started to make loads more happy memories together. We went on several holidays, he taught me how to kayak and to fish and introduced me to camping, which I loved at first but then went off it, so we started going on more luxurious holidays. His kids loved me, my family loved him, and we were so in love with each other. After a few months I let my Gracie and Jimmy move into my flat and I moved into Nick's house with him; they had been together for years but had always lived apart and they felt ready to give living together a go. I took three months off work and worked like crazy, twelve-hour days, to get Nicks house, inside and out, looking so much better. There was only the kitchen and bathroom left to do, which I was incapable of doing, so I got a new job. I was worn out and wanted to go back to an office job for a rest! I was so proud of how I transformed that house and his kids loved it too. It was now more like a home. A year later, we moved out of the house and moved into a caravan at St Lawrence Bay. Nick's son Brandon and his partner Olivia moved into the house at 'mates rates,' to enable them to save up some money to put a deposit down on a house. My Scarlet and Doug used to live in a caravan at St Lawrence Bay, and I had always wanted to have a go at living there myself. The caravan park is on the Blackwater, so we were able to carry the kayaks the two-minute walk to the water and it's a great place for fishing too. It's not a holiday camp, although there is a really lovely pub/restaurant just outside, out of earshot, which was ideal for when we had visitors. It was so quiet and peaceful there, we loved it. Fucking cold in the winter, but I'm in my menopause so I'm hot all of the time and Nick gives a great cuddle, so that never bothered me.

Our caravan had a bit of history, so we got it at a bargain price. The plan was to start with a cheap one and if we enjoyed the caravan life, we'd buy a new one in a year or two. The one we bought was known on the site as 'the incident caravan'. The previous owners were a couple that liked a drink, a bit too much, and used drugs too. They were forever getting shit-faced and would have very loud arguments late at night. One night it got out of hand and he gave her a dig in the head. She fell on the lounge floor and he fucked off to bed. A few hours later he emerged from the bedroom to find her still lying on the floor where he'd left her. He called the emergency services and she was taken to hospital, via the wonderful Air Ambulance, but died when she got there. So very sad. He'd also smashed her head into the wall of the dining area. We knew this because the hole was still there, as was the carpet that the forensic people had cut a large square out of, I assume that was where she had fallen.

Even though we were now living in the 'Amityville' caravan, that we had now done up by the way, life was amazing except for one thing but it's a biggie! I must point out that I do realise that there's no such thing as a perfect relationship. There's always going to be loads of stuff that a couple dislike about each other, but I am also well aware that we just live with all these little things because we love our partners. I ended my marriages and untold relationships in between, because of behaviour that was simply 'unacceptable'. I am, in fact we all are, way too special to put up with behaviour that makes us miserable. I refuse to be in a relationship where I am being bullied by their family, being asked to have group sex, watching them pick their nose and wipe it on my sofa, them not wanting to have sex or cuddles with me, them wanting to put their willy up my bum-hole or leaving fudge marks on my nice clean sheets because they couldn't be bothered to wipe their arse properly and I won't accept them wanting to have sex with other men, or women, and being beaten-up don't do it for me either!

Now call me old-fashioned if you will, but that's just me. What could possibly go wrong between me and the love of my life; my gorgeous, sexy, funny, affectionate, adorable Nick? We obviously had the odd argument. I wasn't keen on him having a poo with the door open and I think my farting got on his nerves a bit, as did my over house-proudness but we were having so much fun together, especially on our weekly Friday night 'date nights' when we would play cards, drink rum, have music on and dance like a couple of nutters around the lounge, whilst singing, laughing and talking utter bollocks. It was great. I hadn't laughed so much since I had been with Gavin. Nick was also so good when I had teary moments, that were due to the overwhelming waves of emotion that I get at times when I miss my Mum and Dad because, he had also loved them very much, so knew just what to do and say to get me smiling again. We had very little dramas with either families so happy days you would think! Except, for some unknown reason, if we were in the company of others, with the exception of our best friends Harry and Marie, he treated me like a cunt! How, and why, did he go from being so wonderful and almost drowning me with love and affection to being so nasty? I can deal with any emotion with ease, but I do struggle with feeling embarrassed. He not only used to embarrass me, but the people that witnessed the verbal abuse too.

The first time it happened was in front of his friend Kevin and his wife, Carole, who had showed up at Nick's house with no warning which, I must admit, I'm not a big fan of especially when we were in total chaos packing to go on a camping holiday. We had just got in from work and only had a couple of hours to get sorted before having an early night coz we were gonna leave at 4 o'clock the following morning. Kevin and Carole knew this but wanted to come round to wish us a happy holiday. When Nick answered the door to them, I was sitting in the garden quickly stuffing my dinner down me before cracking on. Unfortunately, I had taken my bra off, but I did still have my top on of course. When the three of them joined me in the garden Nick had a face like thunder. I assumed he was angry with our unannounced visitors, but it soon became apparent that it was me that he was pissed off with. He snatched my dinner plate away from me and starting shouting at me saying that I didn't have time to eat because we had too much to do. It was then that I twigged what was going through his mind; he was frightened that Kevin and Carole would see my old bangers! He had no worries on that score coz I was sitting down so they were happily resting, out of sight, on my lap! I stood up and went upstairs and put my bra back on. When I re-joined the group, Nick was still angry with me and continued talking to me like shit. It was so bad that Kevin pulled him up on his attitude, which calmed him down a bit. Kevin and Carole are a smashing couple and I used to really enjoy their company, but they always tended to show up without texting or phoning first to see if we were free. Please don't think I am being antisocial, but Nick and I have such busy lives and my diary is always full, every day, normally three weeks in advance with things I need to do and with planned visits to family and friends. Every time they showed up, I obviously had other commitments and would have to try to reschedule, and that is not an easy task. They once came round when I had scheduled a duvet day into my diary, seriously, for the first time in literally years! Again, they were aware that we had flown in from our holiday to Cape Verde at 2am the day before and then had moved back into the caravan after having stayed at my sister's for two months whilst our caravan park had shut down for the winter, and that we were going back to work the following day, but they fancied popping in, so they did. They no longer talk to me because they felt that I was rude to them that day, but I was so exhausted because we'd had the maddest couple of days, both mentally and physically, and we'd had hardly any sleep. I was really enjoying my mega-rare duvet day; Nick and I were lying on the bed watching a film, it was great. I was actually relaxing for once and was all snuggled into my man's lovely big arms when there was a knock on the door; so that was the end of that then. They had not only put a stop to us chilling but also, I need a bit of time to get my head in the right place before we get visitors because I know that Nick is about to change and I have to brace myself for the forthcoming abuse. I shot out of bed and got in the shower. I wasn't going to bother having one that day, but I thought I better had now in case I was kicking up. After I had got dressed, I greeted them with a kiss and a hug, made them tea, got the biscuits out and asked how they and their kids and grandkids were doing. Kevin asked how our holiday was and how the move had gone. Everything I said in response to the questions, Nick disagreed with me so, after being contradicted for about ten minutes I made my apologies and took our holiday washing over to the camp's laundrette. Kevin and Carole thought that was very rude of me and Nick informs me that they will never talk to me again. What a shame, I miss their company lots.

Basically, the problem was that in company, Nick disagreed with everything, and I mean every single thing, that I said. He also criticised everything that I did; right down to how strong I had made the guest's cups of tea to how I was sitting and even the volume of my voice. If I answered a guest's question, for example, when Kevin had asked me, 'How was your holiday?' to which I replied, 'Sorry to say but it was a bit shit really, the food was terrible.', Nick was straight in there and said, 'No it wasn't, it was a good holiday and the food was okay.' We didn't eat for forty-eight hours on that holiday because the food was simply inedible! He would contradict absolutely everything I said, making me look like a liar and a fool. This had happened so much that in the end, I didn't want to be in his company unless we were on our own or with Harry and Marie.

A while back, it was Easter and Nick had said to all his kids that we would both be at the caravan from Good Friday morning until Easter Monday evening, so they could come visit us at any time. I got loads of food and booze in and was really looking forward to seeing them. The pending chaos of them all turning up at different times, sleeping wherever they could find space and being the hostess with the most-est was very appealing. It was going to be like my Mum and Dad's house when I was a kid. My parents both had huge families and we would often have literally dozens of people come stay. I loved it. I'd even enjoy the tidying up when they'd gone, getting everything back in its place and that. There was just one thing that I wasn't looking forward to and that was how Nick was going to talk to me in front of them.

On our date night, that had been moved forward to the Thursday because it was going to be Good Friday the next day, I had a chat with him. I told him that I really was at the end of my tether with his behaviour towards me in public and said that if he was horrible to me in front of the kids, even once, the ice was already very thin and it would crack and that would be us finished; I was deadly serious. He didn't react to my comment and just wanted to carry on with the fun of date night but no, he had to understand that I was serious, so I carried on. I asked him why he thought that he turned into a narcissistic prick when other people were around. Was it because I was funnier than him? Or was it that his kids liked me a bit too much and he was perhaps a bit jealous? He said that he thought he did it because he wanted his children and all of his family and friends to like me, and sometimes, I start showing off in front of them, getting loud and launching into one of my funny stories and he gets nervous. He is so afraid that they might not like me. I got that, I am a bit like Marmite, you love me or hate me, and I suggested that he could look at it another way. His loved ones may think I am too loud, or annoying even, but they love him so much, they are surely just happy to see him happy, so perhaps not to worry so much about what they think of me. I was delighted with his reaction; he so totally got it, thank fuck for that. We carried on with date night and were both really looking forward to the weekend ahead.

Easter couldn't have gone any worse if he had smashed me in the face with a frying pan. It was awful from start to finish. The only bit that I enjoyed was when Nick went to bed on the Saturday night, he had a cold, and left me playing drinking games with some of the kids and their partners. We had a great laugh because the grumpy twat wasn't there. On the Sunday a few of us were sitting outside the caravan drinking coffee after the magnificent fry-up I'd just done us all, when Brandon mentioned that he'd had to tow a mate's car the week before. This made me remember a funny story, from many years ago, which involved their Dad and my old Dad. I was telling them about the incident from 1980's, they were all laughing but then Nick said, quite aggressively 'Can you speed the story up, you're boring everyone.' Brandon jumped to my defence and told his Dad off. I instantly stopped 'boring' them, and went inside, I was so upset.

Two of Nick's granddaughters came to see us on the Monday, they were twelve and seven, and Nick practically ignored them. He was sat in the lounge for two hours looking at Facebook on his phone. The seven-year old really loves her Grandad and was trying so hard to get his attention but he didn't respond, poor kid. I had seen this lots of times before. I think he might think that he looks like a cool Grandad, sat there all moody playing with his phone like teenagers do. Of course, he just looks like a stupid, ignorant, uncaring twat. Not once, the entire Easter period, did he touch me, talk to me civilly, show me any affection or thank me for doing all of the cooking and tidying up, but what he did do was talk to me like I was a piece of shit every time he opened his mouth. Oh well, if you're gonna do it, do it in style I say. The ice was no longer thin, Nick had smashed it to fuck with a sledgehammer; well fucking done. That's ya lot. Here we go again... UN-FUCKING-ACCEPTABLE. Goodbye. I moved out a few days later with just a suitcase of clothes. I left all my furniture, bedding, towels, knick-knacks etc., behind in the caravan, he was welcome to them. I was back to having nothing again; well done me! My eleven-month temping contract was coming to an end on the Friday, so I was now jobless as well as homeless. Gracie and Jimmy were still living in my flat and they were obviously getting on very well indeed because they'd just had little baby Henry so there was no way I was gonna make them move out because that wouldn't have been fair. I was lost, crushed in fact, and didn't know what to do. I was close to madness and didn't like it one little bit. I had been telling everyone for months that I was going to take a couple of months off work and write my autobiography. Nick's kids and my nieces were always teasing me about it and suggesting bits to put in it, bless them. Many people have said to me over the years that I should write about my wonderfully eventful life, but I never really thought that I would get the chance to ever actually do it; life is always just so busy but now, fuck it, why don't I go for it? Also, everyone says that if you are depressed, and I was certainly that, you should write about your emotions, apparently it cleanses the soul. What did I have to lose?

On the Saturday I flew to Spain, my second home. This was the only country that I could afford to rent a place to enable me to be on my own for a while, which I really needed to be. I was proper mental and some. I spent four weeks of my life crying lots, pining for Nick, feeling so angry that he had fucked it up and sitting at the dining room table in my little Spanish apartment, writing this book. I had never been on my own for so long with nobody to talk to before, but it was okay. I only turned my mobile phone on every other day for a few minutes, just to check my messages because I just wanted and needed total solitude. I lost lots of weight, which I needed to, got a little tan, walked for many miles along the beach every day and managed to get myself to relax. It was wonderful, especially the reminiscing bit whilst writing. I think that I did cleanse my soul and got shot of lots of inner anger. I did get a few text messages from Nick when I first got to Spain, but not once did he ask me how I was or if I was safe. He just informed me of how unhappy he was and how I had ruined his life. He truly believed that he had done nothing wrong and that we had split up because I wanted to go to Spain to write a book. I tried to tell him that he had destroyed our, almost perfect, relationship which is why I went to Spain and that I had started to write a book to save my sanity. He would not listen, he was right, I was wrong, end of.

I did a lot of soul-searching during those four weeks and concluded that being loved is not the be all and end all; it's being cared about that matters. I had, and have got, so many people that love me and that's wonderful, but I haven't got that many that actually care about me. That doesn't mean that they're being horrible, it's just that most people are so wrapped up in their own little worlds that they don't see that I am not always the happy, strong, independent person who is available to be there to help them out all of the time. Most of my lot think, 'good old Jackie will help me with that', not realising that they are just one of my many loved ones and sometimes I need a bit of time to myself. Nick loved me to the core but didn't care about me; sad but true. I didn't wait a lifetime for him to then be treated so badly by being humiliated in public. I really wanted to stay in Spain for another four weeks, but I couldn't because I had managed to spend almost all of my savings when I was with Nick, not at his request you understand. I was just a mug with my money during my relationship with him. You see he worked such long hours so

I used to buy all of the shopping, fags and drink because I had more time to do it, but before I knew it, ten grand had just gone. I had to go back to the UK; I had no choice. My plan was to get a temporary job when I got back, stay at Chrissie and Malcolm's again and wait until Gracie and Jimmy got a place, which should be before Christmas and then sell my flat and spend all my money on living abroad. I didn't know where, but it would have to be somewhere where I could legally get a job because I like working; how mad is that?! Before I had even got back to Essex my dreaded diary had got loads of dates in for visits and commitments, but I knew that I was going to find it impossible to slip back into my old life and remain happy. I just wanted to fuck off and live my life the way I wanted to. Nick was, and will always be, the love of my life. Whatever was going to happen in the next few months, at least I could say that I did finally get him, even if it did go tits up!

I found it very hard to say goodbye to my Spanish apartment, I really did feel at home there. I know that I was only in it for twenty-eight days but I had enjoyed being on my own and had experienced a roller coaster of emotions in that time, some good, some bad and I didn't feel as though I was ready to go back into the real world just yet, but needs must and all that jazz. On the coach to the airport I even had a little cry, unheard of for me in public, thank God I had my sunglasses on to hide the tears or I would have looked a right prat. I had a word with myself during the flight home and started to think about the bad bits of being all alone in Spain and the positives of going back to the UK. I wouldn't miss the prickly heat that I was covered in most of the time, all over my legs, arms and a bit on my face, beautiful. Me and the sun have never got on too good, I have the curse of ginger skin and sweat like a pig most of the time at the moment, even when it isn't hot, due to the menopause, not a great combo. When I put sun cream on, which is a must for me, I'm okay until I have a hot flush, my pores then seem to open as far as humanly possible and suck it all in, then my ginger skin gets pissed off and starts getting all red and angry, then insists that I vigorously scratch the cream off, along with a few layers of skin. It seems there isn't an antihistamine that's been invented yet, to stop me waking up in the night with an overpowering urge to rip my skin off! Perhaps I should have gone somewhere less sunny than Benidorm in May! It had been unusually hot for that time of year and everyone else in the resort seemed to be delighted about that, except for me. I did have air-conditioning, which was great during the day, but I couldn't have it on all night because, I knew from past experience from when I had gone to Dubai with Brian, if I had, I would of got a chronic ear infection.

I had picked my apartment because I know Benidorm quite well and it was in the perfect location for my needs, plus it was the ugliest building in Spain, very 1970's, twelve stories high and made out of bland grey concrete, so it was dirt cheap. The inside was nice, basic and in need of a slap of paint, but clean and it ticked all my boxes. There was a nice little kitchen area, that was a must, because I had no intention of eating out. Not only was I skint but I seem to have one of those faces that say 'Please talk to me, tell me all about your boring life and share all of your problems because I'm very interested and have nothing else to do with my time'. Eating nothing but healthy food, exercising lots and leaving the wine alone was on my agenda, but making new friends certainly was not. My new place was quite a good size and from my large balcony I could see the sea, although of course there was only a little bit that was visible, due to the hundreds of hotels in the way, but I could walk to the seafront in just five minutes. When I exited the hideous building and turned right, it would only take me ten minutes to get to my favourite part of Benidorm, the Old Town. None of the low-life go there, just the Spanish locals so the atmosphere is wonderful and the smells from the restaurants make you realise that you are, in fact, in Spain. If I turned left, the famous Benidorm strip was just under a ten minute walk away. At night I could see the bright lights that illuminated the strip, but I couldn't hear it, perfect, so I thought.

The last time that I had walked past my new home was with my William, just a few years before, and I had noted then that, although the apartment block was not pleasing to the eye, it was in a nice quiet area. There were a few restaurants outside it, but they were respectable places that served good food and not the type of cheap, greasy shit that the pissed-up Brits would find appealing. Much to my horror, when I arrived this time, the first thing I clocked was the Sports Bar that had been recently built opposite where I was going to be living for the next month! It wasn't open when I got there, it was before midday so no point in them opening that early because the type of customers they got were still in bed lying in a pool of their own vomit, probably next to a total stranger that they had picked up and shagged the night before. However, I knew that it was gonna be a fucking nightmare of a place by early evening and into the wee small hours, I could hardly wait! I was right, the fun began about 4pm.

It was a Saturday when I arrived, so there were just groups of lads outside the bar at first, shorts on but no shirts, most with big guts, beers in hand, standing outside shouting at the massive television screens that were scattered around the bar. The average age of the loud, drunken, foul-mouthed scumbags was mid to late twenties, with a few token old boys in the stag party groups, who always looked very out of place and you can just tell that they were thinking 'Why the fuck did I let these young idiots talk me into coming away with them?'. Most of the stag and hen parties seem to find it hysterically funny to dress up in various costumes; policewomen or naughty nurses seem to be a favourite for the girls but the boys tended to go more for an Hawaiian or cowboy theme. You could guarantee, with the stags, that the poor groom would be dressed as a woman or have some sort of bondage gear on, normally a gimp mask and some leather straps. Most of the

346

time these groups got right on my nerves, but I must confess, some of their outfits did make me chuckle. I'm such a miserable old mare really but I just don't get fancy dress, I like to feel comfortable when I go out and not like a twat.

Me, Brian, Chrissie and Malcolm went to one of those silly do's once, it was a 1970's theme so Brian added a mullet wig to his outfit. It did look funny because Brian was a baldy so it was amusing, especially as he wouldn't leave his newfound hair alone, he kept twirling it in between his fingers, flicking it and gently moving his fringe to one side. Towards the end of the night, the host approached Brian and said that he could remove his wig now if it'd make him feel more comfortable, then he looked at Malcolm and said the same to him. Malcolm's face was a picture, he was proper insulted because he didn't have a wig on, he's had his natural mullet since the 1970's!! Poor Malcolm, but he had to laugh in the end though. He still hasn't had a haircut mind, despite the fact that I'm forever telling him to! Good on him, he should feel proud that he isn't bald like most of the men his age. I really have been to way too many a party where I have been forced to go out and buy or hire some silly outfit, so not to look like a killjoy, it's very annoying. I even went to a fancy-dress funeral once, seriously, I drew the line with that one, whatever happened to tradition!

The fun and games in the Sports Bar really kicked in at about nine o'clock on that Saturday night, after the football had finished. I'd had an early start, having left to get to Southend airport at around six in the morning, then the journey to the apartment, unpacking, shopping and finally getting to do myself a bit of tea. I was exhausted and just needed to get some kip. I had absolutely no bleedin' chance of that because the football had been replaced by music blaring out of the speakers (inside and outside) of that fucking Sports Bar. The female holidaymakers had now started to show up, most of them looking like prostitutes and obviously on the hunt for a suitable partner to shag. I know I had a bitch about the lot in fancy dress, but this next mob were even worse. Skirts up their arses, tits hanging out and already pissed and proper loud. Most of the blokes had already been there boozing it up for hours so they were now either falling all over the place and getting argumentative or jumping up and down, which I assumed was some form of dancing whilst singing at the top of their voices to get attention from the girls. It was like watching a wildlife documentary, even though, I must point out that animals are far more pleasant to watch when they embark on their mating rituals. It never ceases to amaze me when girls giggle when a total stranger grabs their arse and there was a lot of that going on. Did they honestly think that it was a sign of affection, again I just don't get it! Inevitably, there were a couple of punch-ups between the blokes later, and a few tearful dramas with the girls, the usual. I managed to get to sleep at three o'clock in the morning and this was how it was every night that I was there. I did buy some earplugs after a few days, but they didn't help much and made my ears itch, so I gave up on that one.

The thing that amazed me the most, was how many holidaymakers seemed to be named Dean. There must have been hundreds of different groups of people that came and went, in that four weeks but I guarantee, there was always a Dean. I know this because at the peak of every night's madness, I would hear several blokes chanting, very loudly, over and over again 'DEEEEEEE NOOOOOOO.' Never any other name, I swear, always bloody Deano! Very strange. The thing that pissed me off the most, was how often I heard two particular songs; Neil Diamond's 'Sweet Caroline' and the Oasis song 'Don't Look Back in Anger.' If I walked along the seafront during the day or along the strip of a night, I heard those songs coming out of the various bars, at least every two minutes. Unbelievable. I realise that many of their customers were from the north of England, so probably Oasis fans, but where did they dig that old Neil

Diamond song up from? I used to love that song, but the pissheads had ruined it by shouting 'SO GOOD, SO GOOD, SO GOOD' after the lyric 'Good times never felt so good.' Idiots! I also used to like the Oasis track too but now when I hear it, all I can see in my head is stupid pricks, almost falling off of chairs or tables, cuddling each other in a drunken fashion, doing over the top actions and screaming 'SO, SALLY CAN WAIT.' Oh fuck off!

The thing that amused me the most was my very few walks along the strip of a night. I didn't do it often but some nights the Sports Bar was unbearably noisy so I figured, if you can't beat them, join them. When I had worked in Benidorm in the 1980's, it was in one of the bars along the strip, so I had to take a look at that. I didn't even stay in there long enough to have a drink because I had an overwhelming feeling of sadness when I walked in. I loved working there, back in the day, but going back made it hit home, just how old and cynical I was now, so I left and went into the bar next door and couldn't believe my eyes. They had a new 'Sticky Vicky' and she was just about to start her act. Up until a few years ago, the original 'Sticky Vicky' had been the talk of the resort. She had been entertaining the holidaymakers in Benidorm, seven nights a week, at least six performances a night, all year round from when she was in her early twenties, until her early seventies! She was a fucking legend I tell ya. I was delighted that someone had been brave enough to follow in her footsteps. The new girl was about twenty-five, a lot bigger built than the tiny Vicky but she was also Spanish, went from bar to bar every night to do her thing and her act was almost identical to her predecessor. Watching her brought back some great memories, it's not so much what she does during her act that tickles me, but it's more the joy of observing the people that are watching her, especially the ones who had never seen her before. It's basically a magic act but instead of pulling things out of a hat, she pulls them out of her noony. I realise that it sounds disgusting, but it really isn't. I told my parents to go and watch her when they were in Benidorm, years before, because I knew they would both see the funny side of it, and they did. She pulls all sorts out; twenty foot of bunting, a magician's wand, bunches of flowers, a string of razor blades and, the old classic, a rabbit (a stuffed one of course). She also opens a bottle of beer down there and the grand finale is when the lights go out and she puts a light bulb in, and it lights up. Like the original, she always picks a couple of people out of the audience, the ones with the most disapproving looks on their faces, to check if the beer bottle and light bulb are real before using them. I do love a 'Penelope Pinch-face' look and it's a dead cert that you'll see a few of them in an audience watching that magic show! It isn't as crude as I'm making it sound; she does extract the items discreetly, well, as discreetly as you can when you're standing naked on a stage. There's music playing that she jigs around to and she makes cheeky gestures while she's at it, very entertaining, believe me.

While I was on that plane on the way back to Essex, I managed to think of a few bad bits regarding my time in Spain, which did slightly soften the blow of leaving. However, I didn't manage to think of one single positive thing to brighten the prospect of going back to the UK! My friend Debbie came to the airport to collect me; it was a dirty job, someone had to do it, bless her. When she was driving me from the airport to Chrissie and Malcolm's, she said that she felt as though she was driving a beloved pet to the vets to have it destroyed, that was about right! I walked into my sister's house and it was obviously wonderful to see my family, I had missed them lots, but I had an awful night's sleep, my mind was racing. The next morning, I made a difficult decision, one that is totally out of character for me, but I knew that it had to be done. I went to visit Gracie, Jimmy and gorgeous baby Henry and explained to them that I needed to continue to live on my own to keep my sanity intact and asked them how they would feel if they moved into Chrissie's while they continued to wait for their offer of a council place. It was an extremely hard thing for me to do but their reaction was great. As they pointed out, I did originally say that they could live in my flat for twelve months, which was twenty-two months ago. Gracie was close to her parents, as was Jimmy to his mother and father-in-law, everyone was happy, job done. The following week, they moved out of my flat and I moved back in. It was odd being back there, all the memories came back of how happy me and Brian were when we had first moved in and of the times I'd had there with Nick, but I was okay.

I had only been living there for a few days when there was a knock at the door; it was Nick. My heart flew into my mouth and I was rendered speechless and that don't happen very often! He looked as shocked as I was, but he managed to talk. He handed me an envelope and said that he was expecting to give it to Gracie to pass onto me. There was a bit of an awkward silence but then I asked him what was in the envelope. He explained that he felt uncomfortable that I had left all my belongings in the caravan, so he wanted to give me some money to pay for them. I thought that was a nice thoughtful gesture and invited him in for a cuppa. We had a long chat and decided to start dating again.

That was a few months ago and we are still dating; very happily in fact. Nick lives in the caravan and me in the flat and we see each other most weekends and a couple of times during the week. So far, so good. We have no plans to live together because we are happy the way we are, at the moment. I have given up making long term plans because I find it hard to deal with things when they don't go as I expect them to. That's been my downfall in the past and I ain't gonna make that mistake again. Nick and I feel positive about our future together so, watch this space and time will tell...............

I know that I've got a fucking cheek, because I am shit at making relationships work, but before I sign off, I would like to offer a bit of advice. It's for any single men who have got kids, who are lucky enough to find a barren, orphan who is as excellent as I am, please stop worrying about what your kids and family think of her, just think about how you feel about her, take care of her, let her take care of you and simply play nice and a lifetime of happiness, great sex and shitloads of laughter will be yours for the rest of your life.

Good luck.

The   End

Printed in Great Britain
by Amazon

25994660R00198